HER SAPPHIRE BLADE

A GUARDIANS OF CAMELOT PORTAL FANTASY NOVEL

SARAH BIGLOW

For information contact; www.sarah-biglow.com

Edited by: Under Wraps Publishing Services

Cover Design by: Deranged Doctor Design

Published: 2024 Sarah Biglow

ISBN: 978-1-955988-33-9

10 9 8 7 6 5 4 3 2 1

 Created with Vellum

FROM THE AUTHOR

Special Thanks to:
Jeffrey.Tristan.Thyme, Monica Leonelle, Adriana Anger, Scott Casey, Ryan James, Vicki Hsu, Molly Zenk, Lorenzo, Michael W. Kerr, Melissa Showers, Gerald P. McDaniel, Finley Ymir, Melanie B., Sara Vath, Niels Starfari, Stephen Ballentine and Kaytea Grounds.

ONE

Rain had driven more people than usual into the warmth and ambiance of The Witching Hour, London's go-to bar for magic practitioners and the curious out-of-towners drawn in by the name. Those of us with powers didn't have to hide who we were here. Well, at least not entirely. Big shows of power were frowned upon by the owners. Wards were in place to keep any possible destruction to a minimum. Just enough was allowed to make the tourists think we were just an act to draw them in and relinquish their money.

The usual dull roar of patrons enjoying a drink out with friends was amplified tenfold tonight. The cacophony made my head throb as I stood behind the bar, trying to keep track of incoming orders.

Every available inch of space at the bar was occupied, even though there wasn't enough stools to accommodate the number of people crammed in.

"Oy, Morgan, get your head out of your arse. I asked for those pints five minutes ago," Dean shouted at me, snapping his fingers in my face.

I looked at the server long enough to register what he wanted and pivoted, filling two beer glasses and passed them over. "Sorry," I muttered, but he couldn't hear me over the noise.

Tending bar in London was not where I had thought I'd be as I approached thirty. Yet here I was, busting my ass for tips and still living at home with my aunt. I'd much prefer to live on my own. However, Aunt Nim's health was on the decline and there was no way we could afford to hire someone to care for her full time.

The front door opened and a gust of damp air blew through, sending shivers down my spine. Something just didn't sit right with me today. I could write off the ache in my temple to the weather, but this odd sense of dread had followed me all damn day. Something bad was coming and I couldn't see what it was.

Not that I could do a damn thing about it, even if I could see it coming. I might technically be a witch.

I could feel the power in the world around me, but I was practically useless otherwise. I understood the general mechanics—magic existed everywhere. Magic was basically its own natural force. It couldn't truly be destroyed, just transferred, and remolded into some other purpose. There wasn't any of that good or evil bullshit. It was pure. Only the way a person shaped it made it good or bad. The specific intent was all that mattered.

At least that's how it was meant to work for everyone else. For me, nothing I had ever tried to do went the way I wanted. Even simple things like boiling a kettle for tea goes pear-shaped. Most days, I might as well just pretend I'm mundane like the rest of the world.

Get out of your own head, Morgan.

Wallowing wasn't going to get people their drinks or give me any tips. Forcing a smile, I tugged my shirt into place to best show off my modest cleavage and leaned on the bar. Slowly, the mob at the bar had thinned as people found tables farther in the establishment. The rain appeared to be letting up as the clock ticked past eleven o'clock. I didn't realize until there were only ten people at the bar that I'd been holding my breath. I exhaled and the tension eased between my shoulder blades.

"So, anything decent to drink in this place?" a familiar voice asked from my left.

I pivoted to find my best friend, Julayne Sellers, leaning on the opposite side of the bar. She wore her hair, with the iridescence of an oil slick, pulled up into a knot at the back of her head which only accentuated the sharp contours of her face. Even in the dim light around us, her sapphire blue eyes sparkled brightly. She, like me, was a witch. However, unlike me, she could do some decent shit. It explained how her hair looked perfect right after coming inside from a rainstorm. Though she'd never held it over me or thought she was better than me.

"You know the menu better than I do," I teased as I moved to stand across from her. "But we're running a bit low on most things."

"That's all right. I wasn't that interested in drinking. I only came to steal the bartender."

"I don't get off shift until two," I reminded her.

She let out an annoyed huff. "I can't believe they made you work *today*."

"Come on, Jules, we're not kids anymore. We're grown adults who can manage to work on their birthday without it being the end of the world," I quipped.

"But you only turn thirty once," she whined.

I knew that tone. It was her 'your practicality is ruining my carefully constructed plans' voice. Since we were teenagers, Julayne had treated my birthday like some exalted holiday.

"Get Dean to cover. We are going out," Julayne insisted.

I snorted. "You really think Dickwad Dean would do anything for me?"

She flashed me a mischievous grin. "Oh, he could be persuaded."

"Absolutely not. You know that sort of magic won't fly here. Look, how about this, I'll call Tasha and see if she can come in at midnight. Deal?"

"Fine." She gave an exaggerated eye roll and turned to lean her back against the edge of the bar. "While you're at it, I'll take a bourbon."

I made the drink and slid it over to her on a napkin before scanning the rest of the patrons loitering by the bar. None of them looked like they needed me, so I ducked out the back into the small passageway between the bar and the kitchen. I pulled my phone from my pocket and dialed Tasha's number. It rang five times before going to voicemail.

I didn't bother with a message. Julayne could wait until I got off work. I needed the money more than we needed a girls' night to celebrate another year of my existence on this Earth.

That sense of foreboding washed over me as I hurried along the passage and out back behind the bar. I stayed under the meager awning to keep dry as I sucked in muggy summer air. Rain still drizzled around me. A few drops splashed down on my skin. It felt almost icy, sending shivers dancing up my arm. I focused, pouring all of my energy into summoning my magic. The barest hint of lime tickled my nose as my power sputtered to the surface.

Keep me dry.

The scent grew stronger for a brief moment and I stuck my arm out beyond the protection of the awning. Raindrops fell, but didn't hit my arm. They bounced off an invisible shield, sizzling as if they'd hit something hot.

It lasted for a few seconds before the magic faded and my arm got wet again. I took a few breaths to compose myself. As I turned to go back inside, I could swear I saw someone across the road watching me. I blinked and they vanished. Maybe I just imagined it.

"Get a grip, Morgan," I chided and darted back inside, grabbing a towel on the way to dry off my arm and wipe away the humiliation of another failed spell.

Julayne begrudgingly waited until my shift ended at two. It didn't hurt she'd ordered three more bourbons while she hung around either. She could drink most people under the table. I suspected she used magic to give herself an advantage. Still, four drinks in meant she was already a little tipsy and any filter she'd had vanished.

"You can't hang around after closing," Dean said, making shooing gestures.

"Sod off dickwad," she snapped, flipping him off. "I'm waiting for the birthday girl, so why don't you show some respect."

"It's fine, we're going anyway," I said, closing out the till and stowing my tips for the night in my bag. I rounded the bar and looped an arm through Julayne's.

"See you tomorrow," I called as I dragged Julayne out of the bar and onto the street.

"We better not be going home," she said, sounding offended at the notion.

"Jules, I just worked an eight-hour shift on my feet. I just want to go home and sleep," I answered.

"But it's your birthday. We need to have some fun."

"I'm just not in a celebratory mood."

"Let's at least take the scenic route," she grumbled, tugging on my arm.

I obliged her and we walked arm in arm down the street. The rain had finally stopped altogether, but the streets and sidewalks were slick. The few cars still out this late splashed through massive puddles. It was a miracle we didn't end up drenched.

"You know, I think I know why you hate birthdays," Julayne announced as we walked.

"Enlighten me," I said.

"You hate how they remind you of all those wishes you made as a kid that never came true."

For as long as I could remember, Aunt Nim had told me stories of the fantastical kingdom of Camelot with its gleaming castle on a hill. Where one day, she said I would return to claim my birthright as the heir to the throne. For years, I'd wished every night before bed for it to be true. For some portal to open up and lift me out of the reality that I was a shitty witch with no future.

"Like I told you before, we aren't kids anymore, Jules. It's time we grow up and realize they were just fairytales. They weren't true."

"Girl, we are literal witches with magical powers. But you draw the line at magical kingdoms?"

"You may be a witch, but I can't keep a spell going longer than a few minutes ... if I'm lucky."

"That's because you are supposed to be *there*. Not here." She waved her hands wildly around her, upsetting her balance and sending her staggering into the street.

It always amazed me how tightly my best friend clung to this fantasy that I was some exiled princess from a mystical land. If either of us deserved that title, it should be her.

"And Nim knows it, too," Julayne said as I pulled her out of the street.

"She's been getting stuck in the past more these days ..." I said, sadness permeating my tone.

"It's going to be okay," Jules assured me.

We'd reached the unlit half block leading up to Jules' flat and I instinctively picked up the pace. I hated this stretch of road. It always felt as if it was just inviting danger to lurk in the shadows. I heard footsteps behind us where they hadn't been before. I pulled Jules forward. We'd almost made it to her front steps when a knife whizzed by my head, embedding its blade in the mortar of the brickwork framing the door.

"What the fuck!" I spun to see a man approaching, another knife at the ready in his hand.

"Finally, we can put an end to this," he said in a gravelly tone.

Jules pivoted at the sound of his voice and despite her questionable balance thanks to those four bourbons, she looked clear-eyed. "Get the hell away from my friend you perv!"

A rush of air rippled out from her hands and she sent our would-be attacker skittering across the street. I tugged on her elbow, trying to get her inside.

"We've got to phone the police," I urged.

"No shit," she agreed, and dug in her pocket for the keys to the front door. Jules dropped them twice before she managed to get them into the lock.

Our knife wielding psycho had regained his footing and sheathed the second knife. For a split second I hoped he was losing interest. Instead, he flexed his fingers and a bluish glow appeared around each digit until the entirety of both of his hands glowed like the center of a white-hot inferno. The flames lit up his face, revealing a menacing smile as he cupped his hands together and the flame slithered off his skin into something akin to a ball. He lobbed it at us.

I let out an undignified yelp and dragged Julayne down a step to avoid being burned alive. The fireball collided with the brickwork, sizzling against the damp surface. Heat rippled up my back and panic set in as I flailed, trying to feel if it had made impact. My hands came away warm, but I didn't think I was on fire. Yet I heard the crackle of energy behind me.

"Go, go, go!" I yelped.

I glanced back to find him charging at us with a second fireball raised. It flew through the air, landing on the opposite side of the door from his first attempt. He reached for his belt, except rather than a knife, I could swear he had a fucking sword. I shoved Jules through the open doorway and slammed the door shut behind us, jumping away from it as I heard the solid 'thwack' of the blade striking against wood.

"Who the hell is this guy?" Jules shouted as we thundered up two flights of stairs to her unit.

"How should I know? I've never seen him before," I replied as I struggled to free my phone from my pocket and dial the police. I had to stop myself from dialing 9-9-9 for the mundane authorities. Regular police couldn't do a bloody thing against this magic-wielding psycho. Lucky for us, practitioners had an elite unit who dealt with magic-based crimes.

My heart thundered in my chest as the line rang. And rang. No one answered. For a moment, I was worried we were stuck in a nightmare where every stupid horror trope that scared the life out of me happened all at once. *Please don't let there be skeevy blokes in masks too.*

"Police, what is your emergency?" a disinterested female voice finally squawked in my ear.

"Oh, thank God. Please, you've got to send help. There's a man with a knife, or maybe a sword. And he's been throwing fireballs. He just tried to kill me and my friend," I said in one long breath as I trailed Julayne inside her flat.

"You said a sword, Miss? And fire?"

"Please, you've got to send someone."

I moved to the front window and peered down at the street. Our assailant stood watch and sure enough he sported a sword in his hand. I could even make out the afterglow of the flames he'd been handling. "It is definitely a sword."

"Are you somewhere safe?"

"I ... I think so."

"And what is your name, Miss?"

"Morgan. Morgan le Fey."

She rattled off my address—likely because it was associated with my mobile number. "Is that right?"

"Yes ... but, no ... that's not where I am," I said, fear and adrenaline making my words come out too fast.

Julayne snatched the phone from my hand and provided the proper address. She placed the call on speaker before setting the phone onto the table in the center of the room while we waited for the police to arrive. I kept glancing out the window to find our assailant simply waiting and leaning on their sword as the tip dug into the concrete.

"What's he waiting for?" I muttered, straining to pick up any hint that the police were in fact on their way.

On the table, my phone buzzed with another incoming call. I scooped it up, ready to decline the call when Aunt Nim's name flashed on the screen. My heart leapt into my throat and I couldn't breathe. I fumbled to accept the call and put the police on hold.

"Aunt Nim?" I croaked out.

All I heard was ragged breathing on the other

end of the line, followed by a loud crash. The world flew off its axis and I couldn't remain upright. I slumped to the floor, the phone thudding on the hardwood.

"They ... found us." Nim's voice was weak and breathy.

"Aunt Nim, I'm here. Who? Who's found us? What is going on?" I clutched the phone tight, holding it close to my face, forgetting in the moment it was on speaker.

"You have to ... have to ... Run!"

The line went dead.

TWO

I was halfway to the door before Julayne grabbed me by both arms and spun me around to face her.

"Did you forget about the psycho standing watch like a creepy executioner down there?"

"Aunt Nim's in trouble."

"I get that, but you can't be serious about going to her."

"She's the only family I've got, Jules. I have to help her."

"She told you to run."

"I'm not abandoning her." I was already formulating my route from here. It was only three blocks away to the flat Nim and I shared. It would be risky, but I had no choice. "Look, I'll take the back stairs, and go the long way round. He won't even see me."

"And what am I supposed to tell the police?"

If they ever bother showing up.

"Tell them I went to find my aunt." It was the truth after all.

Julayne released her grip on my hands and darted across the room to a small table. She flipped open a decorative box and plucked out a tiny can of pepper spray on a keychain, tossing it overhead to me. "Just in case."

"I will call you when I know everything is safe," I said, pulling her into a tight embrace.

Pocketing my phone, I crept into the hall and carefully navigated the stairs down to the back alley that ran parallel to the main street. I paused a moment to settle my nerves before I took off at a brisk walk. I didn't need to arouse any other suspicions by being in a hurry this early in the morning. Jules had some nosy neighbors. As I moved with stealth, I still didn't hear the sound of police sirens.

"Get it together," I whispered to myself as I made the final turn to get to our building.

The moment I set foot in the front hall, it felt *wrong*. Like something toxic had spread over every surface. It made my stomach turn and I had to stop halfway up the stairs to avoid being sick. I gripped the railing to steady myself as the nausea gave way to vertigo. I counted the stairs in my head, keeping my eyes shut as I went. It was enough to allow me to make the trek without falling down three flights of stairs and breaking my neck. I'd walked these steps thousands of times since my childhood. Even without seeing them, I knew to skip the second from the top step on the fourth-floor landing to avoid the squeak that would have otherwise revealed my presence.

I pressed my body against the wall, slinking down past the neighbors' doors one by one. I held my breath as I reached the far door at the end of the corridor, the entrance to our flat. My legs shook and tiny black dots popped in my vision from the lack of oxygen. I sucked in a big gulp of air before I darted through the front door. The kitchen and adjoined living room area was in shambles. Shards of broken pottery lay strewn across the floor, along with shattered glass and discarded cutlery on the kitchen counter. I could see spots of something dark red and sticky on the floor. I couldn't lie to myself. I knew it had to be blood.

"Aunt Nim," I hissed.

No reply.

I moved along the back of the flat towards my bedroom. I didn't dare turn on the light for fear it might alert whoever had turned the front living area into a disaster zone. That sense of wrongness lingered in the air around me. I held up my hand, tugging at my recalcitrant magic to illuminate the area around me.

A faint glow shone from my palm. It lasted just long enough to confirm the room was empty. That left Aunt Nim's bedroom. I was about to back out of my room when I realized that would be a foolish move. So, I pivoted and shuffled as quietly as I possibly could to the next room. I thought I could hear something from within.

Aunt Nim!

I threw caution to the wind and barged in, my left hand groping along the wall for the spot where I knew the switch would be. Light sputtered above me and I immediately regretted it.

Aunt Nim sat curled up against the edge of the bed, a ruined dish rag pressed to her stomach. Her hands were slick with blood and her cheeks were dangerously pale. I couldn't quite explain it, but her ears looked strangely pointed. It had to be a trick of the light or the trauma of being attacked affecting my eyes.

"I'm here," I said, falling to my knees.

"I told you … to run," she said, her voice hoarse.

"Couldn't leave you, now could I?"

She winced when I tried to remove the rag. "I'm sorry … I couldn't keep … you safe."

"That's enough of that. I'm going to get you a clean rag and then we're going to take you to the hospital. You're going to be fine," I said and pushed myself to my feet. I rooted around in the chest of drawers next to the bed, grabbing a clean shirt.

"No … hospital," Nim protested.

Prying the bloody rag from her fingers, I gasped at the nasty looking wound in her belly. It was as if someone had impaled her. At least it looked like a clean cut. Maybe the internal damage wouldn't be too bad.

"Let's get you up. Come on," I urged.

She wouldn't budge. "No … still … here. Forgive me … princess."

"Now you're just talking nonsense." Hot tears blurred my vision as I pressed the shirt to her stomach to staunch the blood.

The front door slammed open and I had to bite down on my tongue to keep from shrieking in response. I wasn't going to let some psycho take the only family I had left from me.

"I'm going to fix this," I whispered, kissing my aunt's forehead.

I focused, pouring all of the focus I had into channeling my magic. The most fragrant explosion of lime I'd ever experienced washed over me and I directed it to the wound in her belly.

Heal her.

The magic wrapped itself around Aunt Nim's body and I removed the rag. The sliced flesh and muscle in her abdomen fought to knit back together, but it just wouldn't heal. Ugh, some bloody witch I was. I couldn't even heal the one person who mattered most to me. Heavy footfalls clomped through the flat and the bedroom door slammed open against the wall.

Psycho sword guy now hovered over me along with another man bearing a similar sword. Except his was stained red with my aunt's blood. Fury mixed with the first taste of grief and I let out a guttural howl. I was on my feet, facing down the two men with my hands balled into fists.

"Come on then, you arseholes. You think you can break in and kill a defenseless old woman and get away with it?"

The man who'd attacked me at Julayne's raised a hand as if to swat away a gnat. Before I knew what was happening, I was two feet off the ground and hurtling toward the wall. I collided against the hard surface with a painful thump and couldn't hold back the groan as my head hit both the wall and the floor when I landed on the ground. Pain radiated down my neck and through my shoulder blades as my vision blurred, going grey around the edges.

"Take her … We'll bring her back with us and take the traitor's body, too?" said the one with the bloody sword.

"His orders were clear. Neither survive," Psycho Number One said.

Fuck if I was going to let these bastards take me out that easily. My magic might be shit, but I could still do some damage. Give the police something to work with. But one word tickled my brain, striking a chord with me a few moments later, more than the rest of his words—traitor.

It sounded like these lunatics knew my Aunt Nim. But that wasn't possible. She was my eccentric Aunt Nim. She'd told me fairy tales even when I was too old for them. She worried about me constantly. She'd even tried to get me self-defense lessons when I was fifteen. I'd laughed her off. Despite that she'd still insisted I go and had driven me every week after school for a year.

Did she know they were coming?

My vision cleared as I lay there on the ground while they debated what to do with me. It was probably the oncoming concussion, but I could swear in the bedroom light, their ears looked different. Pointed, just like my aunt's had looked earlier. But that notion was ridiculous. People didn't have pointed ears.

A word from my childhood filtered to the surface.

Seelie.

In Aunt Nim's stories, she'd always made sure to paint the picture of Camelot with both its allies and its enemies. The most dangerous of those being the Seelies. All she'd ever told me was they were manipulative and powerful. As I looked back, she always got this wistful expression when she spoke of them. Not like they were something she missed necessarily, but maybe sadness for something else she'd lost.

It couldn't be true. Yet, these two men with fucking swords were standing in my aunt's bedroom talking about murdering me. Something unnatural was going on. I needed to get up. I had to fight. For my Aunt Nim and myself.

I rolled onto my side and pushed myself off the floor. My head swam in protest to the change in orientation. Though I didn't have a choice. I tried to gauge which one would come at me first as I swayed on my feet. Maybe I could disarm one of them. Without thinking, I rushed the one closest to me, bringing my left knee up to his groin. The move hit true. He groaned, doubling over, and dropping his sword.

I followed it with a jab to his throat before I scooped up the sword. Except that's where my self-defense skills ended. I'd learned to fend off an attacker who was coming at me to grab me, not how to brandish a medieval weapon.

"You don't even know how to use that, girl," Psycho Number One taunted, brandishing his own blade.

"I don't know where you're from, but here it's rude to call someone 'girl.'"

I was stalling for time and we both knew it. I had no idea what I hoped would happen next. Possibly for the police to come barging in to arrest this loon and his partner in crime. Only I realized in that moment, if police did come charging in, they'd find me holding a bloody sword. Not a good look if I wanted to convince them I was innocent. The longer

I stood there, sword hilt clutched in both hands like the amateur I was, the more my eight-hour shift and being thrown into a wall were catching up with me.

My arms felt leaden and my hands shook from the exertion to keep the blade upright. I tried desperately not to look to my right, to where Aunt Nim lay motionless and ghostly pale. Her hands had fallen away from her wound. The blood had now soaked through the shirt.

"Why are you doing this?" I shouted, not caring that it was nearly three in the morning and I could wake the neighbors.

"Orders," he replied, angling his weapon down. Wait, was that a hint of hesitation in his tone?

"I have no idea who you are, but I promise I'm not who you think I am. I'm literally no one important. I'm a bartender. I work for shitty tips."

"The magic doesn't lie," he replied. "I don't relish taking lives. I can make it quick. You won't suffer."

Bullshit.

"You're mad if you think I'm just going to lay down and let you kill me," I argued, doing my best to raise the sword in a fighting stance.

The blade wobbled in my untrained hands and when I tried to charge at him, he blocked me with barely a flick of his wrist. The defensive move knocked the sword out of my grip, sending it skittering across the floor toward his still groaning partner. I didn't back down. Another grief-fueled howl ripped from my throat as I lunged.

He intercepted me mid-motion, his beefy hand wrapping around my throat. He lifted me off my feet and squeezed. The world greyed out faster this time and my lungs burned from the lack of oxygen. Maybe he was right and it would be quick.

Fight!

I could hear Aunt Nim's voice in my head pushing me onward. If I let this bastard kill me, she'd have died for nothing. I dug my nails into the flesh on the backs of his hands and dragged them across his skin. He yelped as I drew blood, but the bastard didn't let go. I tried to dig in deeper, but it only made his grip tighten. I sputtered as I tried to get any last vestiges of air into my aching lungs before I blacked out.

Going into the light must be a real thing. As this prick choked the life out of me with one hand, and his other hand prepared to run me through with his sword, a blinding burst of light filled the kitchen behind him. What I could see tunneled, narrowing in on what looked like a hazy figure approaching.

Jules?

The sudden lack of pressure on my windpipe shocked me out of dying and I fell to my knees. I coughed, trying to regain my body's normal functions. Around me I could hear the muffled sounds of a skirmish, but I couldn't put the pieces together in my head.

My vision came back to me before my hearing and I caught sight of a red-haired woman waving her hands in some complicated gesture. Both men and their swords vanished from the flat. I felt a sudden displacement of air from their rapid departure, but it took far too long to realize that this woman had just magicked my attackers off to somewhere else entirely. Part of me hoped it was a prison cell or some deep, dark hole with alligators. Big ones.

"We need to get you out of here," the woman said, pulling me to my feet. "I have delayed them for a time, but they will be back. They are nothing if not committed to their cause."

"Not that I'm not grateful for the save, but I'm not going anywhere with you. I don't know you. And what exactly did you do to those blokes?"

"I give you my word, I will answer all of your

questions in time. But right now, we must leave. We have a long journey ahead of us."

"And where exactly is it you think you're taking me?"

"Home to Camelot, of course. I've been looking for you for a very long time."

THREE

I stared at her in stunned silence. She couldn't possibly be serious. Those were just fairy tales, stories Aunt Nim had fabricated to cheer me up as a child. They couldn't really be true. I rubbed at the base of my skull where it had connected with the wall and floor. I pushed past the stranger in the doorway and rummaged in the kitchen cupboard for a glass.

"What are you doing?" she demanded.

I reached into the cabinet to the left of the sink and pulled out a bottle of Scotch, pouring it liberally into the glass. "Having a bloody drink."

"I told you already, they will be back. You are no longer safe here."

I tossed back the contents, slamming the glass

down onto the countertop. The wave of adrenaline was beginning to ebb now, bringing with it the tears I'd managed to keep in check until now. "My aunt is dead. I need a fucking minute."

The woman looked like she wanted to say something, but held her tongue. I poured myself another drink and drained the glass, barely hiding a grimace. Scotch was my Aunt Nim's drink of choice. I preferred a good glass of wine. But it seemed a fitting way to honor her. And it helped take the edge off the fear and anger coursing through me like a flash flood of emotion.

"I am not going anywhere until I know my friend is okay," I said.

"By all means ... ensure your friend's safety."

Somehow my phone managed to stay stowed in my pocket and hadn't broken on impact with the wall. I hit number two on my contacts list and waited as the line rang.

"Morgan? Are you okay? Please say something." Julayne's words tumbled out of her mouth.

"I, uh, I'm okay. But my Aunt Nim ... Jules, sh-she's dead. They killed her." Tears turned my words into a sob.

"Morgan, I am so sorry."

"That psycho from your place. He was here. I tried to fight him off, but I couldn't."

"Tell me how to help."

"I—I don't know … I have to go. I just needed to know you were all right."

I dried my eyes with the back of my hand as I ended the call and stowed my phone. I took some time to study the woman in front of me. Her red hair was darker than I'd first thought, closer to russet than ruby. She wore a simple tunic top over tight fitting pants and leather ankle high boots. If I'd passed her on the street, I wouldn't have thought anything of her.

"Right. Who the hell are you and why do you think I'm from some made up fairy tale my aunt cooked up?"

"My name is Emerys. I am a witch, like you."

"Nah, you're nothing like me. You've got power. I could feel it. I can't even do a simple healing spell. My magic is worse than useless. It's like I—"

"Like you can't feel it."

"Wait a bloody minute … How'd you know?"

"Because your magic was not born of this world. You belong in Camelot." She took a step toward me and for a moment I saw an almost motherly expression in her eyes. "I promise, I will explain every-thing. But we need to leave ... Now."

"We can't leave her here. We've got to notify the authorities."

"We do not have time."

"Give me one reason I should trust you."

"I saved your life."

"Fine. You say we're off to Camelot? Grand. How exactly do you suggest we get there?"

"Do you have a vehicle?"

"We can drive there?" I scoffed in disbelief. If this mystical realm had been within driving distance of London all this time, why hadn't my aunt just taken me there as a child?

She fixed me with a serious expression. "Do you have an alternative?"

"I don't know. We could fly."

It took a moment for my words to register in her brain. "We don't have time to forge me sufficient documentation to access that means of transport. Driving would be easier."

"Tell me where we're headed?"

"Uisneach."

I had no idea where that was so I pulled out my phone again and typed in my best guess of the name's spelling into a search. Ireland? "You want to go to Ireland from here?"

"It is the only portal I am aware of that will take us both to Camelot, and Albion at large."

"You're telling me you came through a portal in *Ireland* and traveled all the way to London to save me, but you don't have a convenient way back?"

"I'm afraid my trip here was one way only. A bit of borrowed sorcery. We will have to use your means of travel to get back to the portal."

This was madness. "Where'd you send those blokes?"

"Here is not the place to continue this conversation. Pack what you can carry. We need to leave."

"But ... I mean, did you send them back to wherever they came from or did you punt them to somewhere like Manchester?"

"Even with my power, I could not expel them from this realm. But they are going to keep coming for you. So, the sooner we are back on Camelot's soil, the safer you will be from them."

"Give me ten minutes to get a bag together."

AFTER TRYING to start Aunt Nim's old junker of a car for ten minutes, I realized driving wasn't going to get us where we needed to go. Well, at least not right away. It was probably for the best. Gas was expensive as shit. I leaned on the boot of the car, studying my phone while Emerys paced nearby watching me.

"Okay, looks like there is a ferry out of Liverpool that gets us to Dublin. Then it's just a few hours' drive from there," I said through a yawn.

"Where is Liverpool?"

"About a four-hour trip from here by train. Probably better anyway. Even if they found us, I don't think they'd want to do anything with all the witnesses on a train."

"Can you make the purchase?"

I held up the phone to show her I'd already purchased tickets for a six o'clock morning departure. It gave us enough time to reach the station and maybe get some coffee.

By the time we arrived at the train station, the sun had risen, reflecting off the windows opposite us. I regretted not packing sunglasses and threw an arm over my eyes to shield them from the sun.

"I am truly sorry we had to meet under these

circumstances," Emerys said softly from her seat beside me.

"Can we not do this right now? I'm exhausted and I've been attacked twice in one night. Can I just get a little quiet? Please?"

She made a yielding gesture and remained silent until our train was called. I led the way to the platform and climbed aboard. She followed after me. Given the early hour, we had most of the train car to ourselves. I drew the shade on the window next to me and curled up as much as I could. I felt her hand on my wrist and a warmth spread throughout my body from her touch.

"Sleep now, child," she whispered.

The sound of the train coming to a halt on squeaky rails roused me. I sat up, groggy and disoriented. Looking around there were more people in the train car now and a man in a conductor uniform moved through the car, collecting tickets.

I wiped the sleep from my eyes and straightened up, holding our tickets out for him as he came by. He punched them, sticking them in two little slots above our seats before moving on.

"Do you feel better?" Emerys sat across from me with her head turned toward the window.

"I don't know about better, but I don't feel like I'm about to pass out."

"Good. Because our Seelie pursuers boarded the train one stop ago."

I craned my neck behind me, but didn't spot either of the sword wielding arseholes. "Are you sure?"

"I did not think they would find us so soon."

"What do we do? We're not even close to our stop."

"It is my hope that they wouldn't want all of the collateral damage. As much as it pains me to say, one dead woman is explainable. A train car full is not something that can be overlooked."

"Why do they want me dead?"

"Because you are the one person who can undo a grievous wrong. You are the rightful heir to Camelot's throne, Morgan. Once you lay claim to your birthright, their farse falls apart."

"What are you even talking about?"

I heard the door at the far end of the car open and my stomach dropped. I didn't want to turn around. I didn't want to see those two men again. Somehow I had managed to not dream of them when I'd fallen asleep earlier. I suspected Emerys was to thank for that. But seeing them now, I wasn't sure I could contain my rage and anger at what they'd taken from me.

Emerys rose calmly and held out a hand to lead me to the next car. Hiding out in another car would only get us so far. Eventually, we'd run out of passenger cars and they'd catch up with us. We might only have a few stops to go, but we couldn't duck them forever.

"How certain are you that they aren't going to start stabbing people?" I whispered as we moved through the designated quiet car.

"Relatively." She didn't sound confident in her response.

"Can't you send them away again?"

"Is magic practiced out in the open here?"

"I mean … it's kind of a poorly kept secret. But people don't go around doing it for the hell of it, no."

"Then I cannot simply make them disappear. It would arouse too many suspicions. Now, come along."

We reached the final car just as the train pulled to a stop, announcing Liverpool. Maybe we'd get out of this without attracting attention, but we still had to make it to the ferry. But it was too much to hope for as we stepped onto the platform and I spotted the two men step off the train with us.

I scanned our surroundings and noticed a cluster of people who looked as though they might be on some sort of trip together. I tugged Emerys along and darted through some of the group's stragglers.

"Sorry," I apologized when one of the women in the group gave us a nasty glare.

We'd just managed to clear through the group outside when I heard someone shriek. The ground beneath my feet shook. Our pursuers weren't afraid to use magic in public. I could see cracks forming in the concrete platform, spiderwebbing out toward the tracks. If they managed to dislodge any of the concrete onto the rails, it could cause derailments or worse. The man closest to me, the one who'd nearly choked the life out of me, was controlling the magic with his hand. It glowed a vivid gold and whenever his fingers twitched, new cracks formed. We were screwed, but still had a ways to go to make it to the ferry. Somehow, I swallowed my nerves. I couldn't afford to break down now. Not when there were so many innocent people around to become casualties of a fight I still didn't understand. Innately, I knew I owed it to these people to try and keep them safe.

"The ferry's just up that way. If you hurry you

can make it," I said, urging Emerys ahead of me. I tried to slip her the money, but she wouldn't take it.

She stayed firmly rooted to the spot when I didn't move. "If you stay, I stay. I spent so many years searching for you. There's no way in hell I am about to leave you behind now." She took my hand and gave it a squeeze. "Now focus. I want you to envision a barrier between them and the people in front of them."

"You want me to do magic. Here. Now. Maybe you didn't hear me before. My magic doesn't work."

"Trust me."

That same warmth spread from her hand to mine and up my arm, settling in my chest. I closed my eyes, letting the feeling of my magic fill me up. It came easier this time. Almost as if it wanted to be used instead of fighting me tooth and nail.

Protect them.

It was like something had ignited inside me. Lime cascaded over me like someone had dumped an entire vat of juice on me. It permeated my every pore and made every nerve ending light up with energy. I opened my eyes and a smoky barrier spanned the length of the train platform.

"Holy shit," I croaked.

The cracks in the concrete slowly closed,

repairing themselves now that my would-be murderers were busy trying to contend with the magic keeping them firmly separated from us. To their credit, most of the civilians didn't notice and just hurried on their way.

"Now, we need to go."

Emerys tugged me backward and I stumbled as I turned to follow her. She never let go of my hand. I looked back to see both men draw their swords and begin slashing at the barrier. It kept them busy long enough for us to make it out of the train terminal and onto the ferry.

The moment Emerys let go of my hand, the energy I'd felt faded and my body ached. I rolled up my sleeve to see faint pink marks, as if someone had cut me.

"Let me guess, magic swords," I sighed. How had I not felt their blows before? Had Emerys taken the pain from me?

"You did well back there. Untrained, yes ... but you have good instincts."

"That's the first time I've ever managed to sustain something like that. And I mean ever." After a moment, I added, "You did something. Lent me your power or I don't know ..."

"I merely gave your magic something familiar to

hold on to. To buttress itself again. You did the rest." She gave me a sympathetic look. "As I said, your magic was born of another place. It recognized that place in me."

We queued to board the ferry and I couldn't help glancing back. The men had to have gotten through the barrier by now. The fact I didn't hear any more shrieks suggested they hadn't taken out their frustration on innocent bystanders.

"Next," a deep bass voice called from the front of the line.

We shuffled forward, paid our fare, and boarded. The moment we set out on open water; I caught Emerys letting out a sigh of relief. There was a lot she wasn't saying. We were about to be stuck on a boat for four hours. Time to get to know my rescuer.

FOUR

The fresh air helped settle my nerves as I found a seat in a secluded area of the ferry. Emery joined me, staring out at the water. After a moment, she turned to look at me, expectation written all over her face. She was ready for my questions now.

Where did I start?

When I was young, I'd had millions of questions that I'd never gotten the nerve to ask Aunt Nim. Now, I couldn't ask her. I'd longed to know how I'd gotten here. Why had we come if I was supposed to rule a kingdom? Were my parents okay? She never talked about them.

"How do you know that I'm the person you think I am?"

"Because magic recognizes like magic. I have always had an affinity for tracing magic in a bloodline and while you may not feel it here, yours is strong. It is the beating heart of a kingdom."

"If I'm so special, why am I here?"

"I do not have all the details, but from what I understand, your mother endured a difficult delivery. She was weak afterward and easily manipulated. She was led to believe her child was in fact born a boy."

I gestured to my very clearly female anatomy. "Pretty sure it would have been obvious I didn't come out with a knob and bollocks."

"It was only your mother and the midwife in the room. I was otherwise engaged. Perhaps if I had been there, I could have prevented what happened."

"How'd I end up here?" I repeated.

"The midwife disappeared, claiming the child needed to be examined. When she returned, she carried a boy in her arms. No one questioned it."

"You lot don't have ultrasound machines?"

"Aunt Nim had always given me the impression that Camelot was a lot like here."

"Technology can be incorrect. Or miss things," Emerys replied.

"So what, this midwife just dumped me some-where and someone found me?"

"No. I believe you were given to a Seelie woman who had orders to kill you. By some miracle she disobeyed those orders and fled the kingdom. She went to the only place she thought she might not be pursued. Through a portal to another realm."

"My Aunt Nim was supposed to kill me?"

"I believe so. But I see now that she gave her life to protect you."

"I don't understand. If she could go through this portal, what stopped those thugs or you from coming after us before now?"

"Magic is a wonderous thing, but it can have a mind of its own. Believe me, I tried to get through many times before now. Perhaps Nim's magic was strong enough to keep you both hidden until now."

"She's been sick. Doctors couldn't figure out what it was. Could it have something to do with her magic fading? Is that even possible?"

"It may very well be."

"Her ears were pointed. Like the guys who attacked us. I'd never seen that before."

"Using magic constantly to conceal one's iden-tity can take a toll on anyone. Perhaps being away from the root of her own power for this long was too much for her."

"She always warned me that Seelies were dangerous and not to be trusted. Why would she say that about her own people?"

"Because it was true."

"Do they know about me? My parents?"

Emerys shook her head, gaze cast down at her hands. "I have not spoken to the Queen in nearly three decades. I tried to convince the royal family you'd been taken, but they refused to accept it. I fear now that they were under the influence of others around them."

"So, I'm supposed to just show up and what ... tell them 'Hi, I'm the daughter you never believed existed. Who wants tea?'"

"You will have to earn a way to an audience with them. Don't worry, I have a plan."

"Hope it's a good one," I said just as the ferry's horn blared to announce we were approaching the harbor in Dublin.

As soon as we disembarked, I could feel something different about the ground beneath my feet. It felt almost familiar. But that made no sense since I'd never been to Ireland before.

Except as a baby.

"Come, we must secure a vehicle for the final leg of our journey," Emerys said.

"Hold on. I've slept maybe two hours and haven't had anything to eat. Before we go anywhere, I am going to need breakfast."

She let out an annoyed huff, but acquiesced. Thankfully, we found a café serving breakfast across from a car rental. Maybe things were looking up. The coffee turned out to be strong and the food was half decent.

"So, who exactly are you?" I said with my hands wrapped around the coffee mug in front of me.

"Once I was an advisor to the royal family. But since your birth I have been something of an exile."

"They just kicked you out all because they didn't like what you had to say? I'm not sure I want to meet these people."

"As I said, I believe they were and are still under the sway of others. But, as I am not permitted on palace grounds, I cannot be certain."

"But you think they'll just let a stranger walk in without a question?"

She gave me a mischievous smirk. "I do indeed."

"But you're not going to tell me about it?"

She looked around the café. "Not until I know

we are somewhere we will not be overheard by prying ears."

"Right … well, then I guess we better get going. It's still a few hours' drive to your mystical portal."

I paid the bill and we crossed the road to the car rental. I didn't have the heart to tell the man behind the counter that he most likely wouldn't be seeing his property again. But maybe there was something Emerys could do to help. Could she make the car drive itself back? He pointed us to a small vehicle at the far end of the lot.

"Just been filled up, too. You're lucky," he called as he tossed me the keys.

I caught them in both hands and started for the driver's side. The keys fluttered out of my grasp and over to Emerys' outstretched hand. "Just because I do not have legal documents in your world, doesn't mean I don't know how to operate one of these."

"Well, excuse me."

I rounded the front of the car and settled in the passenger's seat. Emerys slid behind the wheel and revved the engine. We were already essentially sitting on the road and I flipped on my phone's GPS to direct us where we needed to be.

It became clear very quickly Emerys did not have a clue what she was doing. The road was empty for about a quarter kilometer before other cars appeared. Horns blared angrily as they swerved to avoid us.

"Shit, you drive like a bloody American!" I shouted, making a mad grab for the wheel to force us out of the flow of traffic coming at us in the wrong direction.

"This is the proper side of the road," Emerys argued.

"Pull over."

She eased the car to a stop on the side of the road. "Right, I'm driving before you get us killed."

"Forgive me for trying to do something nice."

I released the seatbelt and climbed out of the car, marching around the front, and yanked open the driver's door. "Thank you, but I've got it from here."

She slid across to the passenger seat and I settled behind the wheel. I waited a count of ten for my heart to settle back into a normal rhythm. Carefully I eased across the road to the correct side and began to follow the map route toward our destination. Silence filled the car. For a while it settled between us, giving me time to process everything.

Aunt Nim was gone. Had someone found her body? Jules knew she was dead. She'd make sure the authorities knew. Or had the Seelie douches done something to her body? They'd caught up with us awfully fast, so I had to assume Emerys hadn't booted them too far away. For all I knew, they could have literally sprouted wings and flew.

"What do you do exactly?" I said when the silence had gotten too deafening.

"I consider myself a teacher. I have one student. An apprentice really. And I help my pupil hone their craft."

"What did you do before that? Before … I was born, I mean."

"I was one of the Queen's closest advisors. I advised her mother before her and her grandmother before that."

"You can't be old enough to have served three generations," I said.

She chuckled. "Looks can be deceiving. But I was there when your mother was crowned."

"Aunt Nim never mentioned you," I said as the GPS signaled that we were only ten minutes away. "She told me all kinds of stories growing up about Camelot. About how the magic worked there, just like here. But it was more untamed. She told me how the Queen was a kind and benevolent leader. She didn't judge people based on where they came from.

She told me that I came from a long line of strong women.”

“All of that is true.”

“But she never once mentioned you.”

“In truth, your mother and I had drifted apart before her pregnancy. I think she felt I was out of touch with what she and her people truly needed.”

“Was she right?”

“You would have to ask her. But I believe there is still hope for our reconciliation, through you.”

“You’re putting a lot of faith in someone who can barely sustain a spell without help.”

“Trust me, you will feel differently once you are back where you belong.”

The GPS beeped, indicating we’d reached our destination. I could see fencing around some rock formations. I spotted a small break in the fence and guessed we’d be sneaking in. I didn’t see any other cars in the vicinity or cameras.

“You’re sure we’re not going to get arrested?”

“We will be gone before anyone notices.” She climbed out of the car and darted around the rear to my side before I even had time to undo my seatbelt. “Follow me.”

The moment I set foot out of the car, I was hit with a surge of magical energy. This place was brimming with untapped magic waiting to be guided. I'd never felt anything like it. It wove around me like a cat looking for attention. Even though I could feel the magic in the world around me, without Emerys boosting my signal, I couldn't connect to it.

"This place is intense," I managed as I trailed her to the break in the fence.

"Great battles were fought in this place a long time ago and the mystical energies from those battles remain," she explained.

We stopped by one of the rock formations and I watched her body language shift. She stiffened and sadness washed over her features. She shed a single tear, wiping it away with her fingertip before moving past the rocks and down a shallow incline.

"How do you know all of that?" I called.

"Because the other side of the barrier is the same. And all things must have balance. Light and dark."

"I'm not going to have to jump off a cliff or something am I? I'm not good with heights."

"Just keep up," Emerys said, walking steadily onward.

I couldn't pinpoint the exact moment the world shifted around me, becoming wholly unfamiliar, but beautiful. One moment, I knew we were in Ireland

and the next, we stood just beyond a cave by a burbling river. Emerys looked unfazed by the transition in terrain.

"Wait up!" I called as she moved ahead.

I stumbled on some loose dirt and had to catch myself on the branch of a nearby tree. When I looked down, I found the tree reaching out to steady me. It had to be a trick of the light or exhaustion catching up to me. But in the back of my mind I'd thought that I could use the help. I hadn't used any magic, but the tree had definitely reached out to keep me from faceplanting.

I let go of the branch and picked my way through brambles until I finally caught up to Emerys. As we walked on, I understood what she'd meant. I could feel the magic around me here, too. It felt welcoming and familiar. I knew I'd never been here before, but it was like the magic knew me and wanted me here. I couldn't help testing out Emerys' theory that my magic would respond to me now that I was allegedly where I was meant to be.

I turned my focus inward and my magic came screaming at me like it had never been truly free before. *That's because it hadn't.* It thrummed against my skin, making my fingers ache as I tried to decide what to do. I spotted a trampled flower on the path ahead and knelt down, cupping it in my fingers. I wasn't much of a gardener, but Aunt Nim had loved flowers.

Grow.

The petals perked up, turning vivid yellow as the stem straightened and the leaves unfurled. And as if that weren't enough, the rest of the flowers next to it brightened and straightened, too. I caught Emerys watching me with a grin on her lips. She apparently liked being proven right.

"This is mental," I said as she led me up the ridge of a small hill overlooking a lush valley. I could see a lake in the distance, separating out two distinct patches of land. The farther area sprawled with rolling hills surrounding a castle of bleached white stone, tiny blue flags were flying from the tops of its darkly roofed towers. I turned my gaze skyward to see the sun beginning its descent along the horizon, painting the sky in calming shades of lavender, burnt sienna, and pink. Even the clouds looked more serene here as the sun set on another day. I could almost hear Aunt Nim's voice in my head, whispering about what the sky would look like once dusk fell and the stars came out.

"Aunt Nim was right, it really is beautiful here," I murmured. My breath caught in my throat at the realization that she would never be buried where she came from. She'd never get to come home again. I let out a sniffle and wiped my eyes. There would be time to grieve later.

I caught Emerys beaming at me as she made a sweeping gesture with her hand. "Welcome to Camelot."

FIVE

I could almost picture an eight-year-old me doing cartwheels down the hill toward the lake with Aunt Nim chasing after me. I could hear her laughter in my head and a fresh pang of loss gripped me, squeezing my chest tight.

"Come, we have a lot to do," Emerys said, placing a guiding hand on my arm.

"You said when we got to Camelot you'd tell me what your mysterious plan was to get everyone to believe I am who you say I am. We're here."

"Don't be so literal or stubborn. There are far too many watchful eyes in these woods to speak openly."

I tamped down my frustration and followed her along the ridge toward the lake. As we walked, I realized just how far the castle really was from our current position. The lake was massive and we navigated part of its circumference for what felt like an hour before a modest cabin came into view partially hidden amongst a stand of trees.

"You live in a log cabin?" I couldn't help but snicker.

"I couldn't serve you if I lived in a tree," she muttered and produced an ornate brass key from her pocket. She slipped it into the lock on the front door and pressed her forehead to the wood.

I could swear the door gave an audible sigh, like it was relieved to have her back, as it opened. She stowed the key and stepped inside. I stayed outside, just taking in the scenery.

"Don't just stand there dallying. Come in," she called.

From within, I heard thundering footsteps and a moment later, a bloke about my age came skittering into view. He had dark shaggy hair that fell artfully above his aquamarine-colored irises. Thin wire-framed glasses rounded out the look. He was kind of handsome in a bookish sort of way. Nothing could have hidden his pure excitement upon seeing me.

"You did it. You really found her," he exclaimed with an accompanying fist pump.

Emerys gave him a disapproving look. He lowered his hand and tried to contain himself. She turned to me and explained, "This is Gethin Westbridge, my student."

"Apprentice, really," he offered.

"Right. Hey." I gave a small wave.

"You're Morgan. I've heard so much about you. Well ... I mean not everything, obviously. But we've been waiting for you to come back for ages," he gushed.

"Gethin, enough. Let the girl take a breath. Why don't you go put something on the stove? It's been a long, trying journey to get here," Emerys instructed.

"Of course. Right. Should have had something ready when you got here."

He darted out of sight. Moments later, I heard the clang of pans against burners. Emerys made another 'enter' gesture. I had no reason to refuse. After all she was offering me food and shelter.

"He's a bit ..." I trailed off.

"I believe the word you are looking for is excitable."

"That about sums it up."

"He's been studying with me since he was fifteen. He's a good lad. Whip smart."

"So, why's he just an apprentice then?"

"Because it takes more than a decade to truly master magic craft."

Gethin appeared—or rather his head and shoulders popped out from behind a doorframe—and he waved a hand to get my attention. "You ... uh eat meat, right?"

"Yeah. I'm good with whatever."

He vanished again, leaving Emerys and I standing in what I assumed to be a sitting room. There were a few oversized chairs next to an empty fireplace. The overhead lights were dimmed and yet I could still see. I wondered how she got electricity out this far in the forest, but figured it was rude to ask. But I couldn't say I wasn't relieved that the place was modern, if a bit on the rustic side. I noted the lack of photos or anything personal on the walls —spartan.

"I suppose I should give you the tour while Geth's busy," Emerys said.

She led the way to a small dining area with a table big enough for four people. I peeked through the open doorway to find Gethin, his back to me, stirring something on the stove. Beside him a knife chopped vegetables of its own accord on a cutting board.

"Give me about twenty minutes," he called, as if he could see me standing there.

I turned and found Emerys waiting at the bottom of a short staircase. "Follow me."

The single flight of stairs led up to a floor with three bedrooms. She stopped at the room at the far end of the hall. "This will be yours for now."

I peered in around her. It sported a small bed and a wardrobe in one corner. A single window overlooked the lake. I set my bag outside the wardrobe, eyeing the bed. I could use some sleep.

"You can rest once we've completed the tour," Emerys said.

"The privy or what you call the loo is that door over there. Fair warning, Gethin hogs the hot water in the mornings."

"So, he's got the sleeping hours of a proper adult, but the courtesy of a teenager. Got it," I said with a small smile.

"One more stop," she said and retreated back down to the first floor.

I couldn't imagine what else she had to show me. The cabin didn't look big enough to house anything more than what she'd already shown me. She stepped out the back door and waved her hand in the air, as if trying to gain someone's attention from a distance.

What had been a wooded area moments before transformed. Tree trunks thickened, blending one into the next to form makeshift walls. Their canopies stretched and wove together to form a roof of sorts. Their roots flattened to form a rough, but even floor.

"This is where you will train." Emerys urged me onward. "It is designed to allow the use of magic, but also ensure you don't injure yourself ... too much."

"Convenient," I said.

"Food's on," Gethin called from behind us.

I stepped back inside and followed him to the table where he'd laid out bread and a pot of stew. It smelled like heaven and I sunk into the chair next to him. "You really made this in twenty minutes?"

He shrugged and ducked his head in embarrassment. "Well, I—I mean ... I'm sure you could have done it faster."

"Mate, you don't ever want me cooking unless you like your food burnt beyond recognition."

Emerys joined us and Gethin let out a nervous laugh. "She's funny. You didn't say she'd be funny."

"It's difficult to gauge someone's sense of humor

before you've actually met them," she reminded him.

My hunger temporarily overrode my desire for sleep and wanting Emerys to explain what plan she was cooking up. I caught Gethin watching me as I shoveled the contents of the bowl in front of me into my mouth. He made a show of adjusting his glasses before turning back to his own meal. The sky outside darkened as we ate and finally the sun set completely. The lights above us brightened in response.

"Can I help clean up?" I offered. "I feel like a terrible house guest otherwise."

"Sure," Gethin replied. We left Emerys sitting at the table since she appeared lost in thought anyway.

I took a quick inventory of the kitchen now that I could stand in it properly. Cleaning supplies sat under the sink, just like I'd expect along with extra dish rags and soap.

"You look surprised," he commented as he handed me dirty dishes to scrub.

"I didn't really think it would be so similar," I admitted. "I figured Aunt Nim just said it was like where I lived, because it would be easier for me to believe. Not because it was true."

"I've wondered what it would be like beyond the barrier," he said and handed me another bowl.

"Nothing fancy. People are generally all right. But you've got your usual arseholes and creepers. People still get sick. They die. I imagine that's what you'd find anywhere you went."

"What about the magic?"

"What about it?"

"Emerys said it was kept hidden. Or it used to be."

"We don't go around wearing signs that say, 'Hi I can do magic.' But it's not like we're going to be hanged for it if people found out. At least not anymore."

"I can't imagine having to hide who you are."

"So, you've been with Emerys for a while now. How's that been?"

"It's been good. Really good. I've learned so much from her."

"Not to be rude, but she told me that she got exiled by the Queen. Why would you want to study with someone who got kicked out?"

"Just because she had a falling out with the royal family doesn't mean she still doesn't know a lot about magic craft. She's been around for a long time."

"How long we talking?"

"Like I'm pretty sure she's at least a hundred years old," he whispered.

"Bollocks."

"I know, she doesn't look a day over thirty-five. But I am telling you, she's been around for ages. It's why she's so good at magic. She's got one of the longest-running connections to it of anyone I've ever met."

"I heard about some other people ... Seelies. What's your take on them?"

"Avoid them when you can. They aren't to be trusted. They think everything should belong to them and they aren't keen on following the rules of etiquette."

"Sounds about right."

"But don't worry, they're pretty easy to spot." He tapped the tip of his ear. "Pointy-eared bastards."

"I'm familiar with a few. They tried to kill me today."

Gethin's face melted into a look of horror. Before he could speak, Emerys appeared. "I think we've given Morgan enough excitement for one day. We have an early start in the morning. You should both get some sleep."

She didn't have to tell me twice. I bounded up

the stairs to the loo and found, much to my relief, that it was a proper toilet and sink. It even had a tiny shower stall tucked into one corner. Apparently, economy of design wasn't a uniquely British thing. I fetched a nightshirt from my bag for after my shower before I hopped in the tiny stall.

The water pressure left something to be desired. Just like home. Thankfully, it was warm and it felt good to wash off the sweat and stink of nearly being murdered twice in less than twenty-four hours. In here, I didn't have to put on a brave face, so I let the tears fall. The sound of the water pattering against the stall door wasn't quite enough to mask the sobs that ripped from my throat as I bent over double, the weight of Aunt Nim's death crashing into me again.

Neither Emerys nor Gethin commented when I stepped out of the bathroom ten minutes later. They just bid me goodnight. I climbed beneath the sheets and prayed I could actually sleep.

To say I slept would be a generous use of the term. I tossed and turned, plagued by recurring images of those sword-wielding bastards coming after me. Sometimes they caught me, running me through just like they'd done to my Aunt Nim. I'd sat up in a cold sweat more times than I could count, my whole body shaking at the sensation. By the time my phone read seven o'clock, I was just starting to drift back to sleep.

"Time to get up," Gethin's voice called through the closed bedroom door.

I let out a groan, ducking my head beneath the pillow.

"I know what you're thinking. It's way too early to get up, but Emerys left strict instructions for us. We've got to test your powers, see where you're at before she gets back."

I waited, hoping he would just leave me alone so I could go back to sleep. Except there was no telltale sound of footsteps on the wooden floor or the creak of weight on the stairs. I dragged myself out of bed, pulled on clean pants and a shirt from my bag, and wrangled my hair into a knot at the nape of my neck. I yanked the door open to find Gethin still standing there in sweatpants and a t-shirt.

"Coffee," I said.

"Already brewed."

I stopped in the loo long enough to brush my teeth before I went down to find what appeared to be freshly baked scones on the table along with a metal carafe of coffee. I poured myself a cup and spread a liberal amount of what turned out to be homemade raspberry jam on my scone. Just like the stew the night before, it was utter perfection.

"You should open a restaurant. You'd make a fortune," I said as I downed the last dregs of coffee from my mug.

"It's just a hobby. Nothing serious. Part of why I'm still studying is because I haven't found what I really want to do."

"I'm telling you, you've got a gift for food," I said as we cleared away the dishes.

"Right, well let's see what you're working with," he said.

He did the same waving gesture Emerys had done the day before and the woods transformed again into the enclosed space. My stomach dropped the moment I set foot inside. I was about to make an absolute fool of myself.

"Let's start easy," Gethin said and pointed to a fallen log on the other side of the space. "Stand that log upright."

That's easy?

I started to walk towards it, but Gethin blocked my path. "From where you're standing is fine."

"But it's really far," I protested.

He didn't move. Just like when I'd used it the first time in Camelot, my magic practically poured out of me when I reached for it. In England it was like I'd been trying to use a hose with a kink in the line. Though now, not only was that kink eliminated, but someone had turned up the intensity to full blast.

Go upright.

I held a hand out toward the log. It shook on the ground, as if possessed, and after a moment, it began to lift upright. Except it didn't stop once it was vertical. My power continued to flow full blast and the log tugged free of the flooring and shot up into the canopy, lodging itself halfway through the branches.

"Uh, well, I got it upright," I said with a sheepish grin.

"Not really what I meant," Gethin said, rubbing at his chin.

"Okay, how about we try something a little more focused. I want you to come at me and try to subdue me without touching me."

"I'm not sure that's a good idea," I said.

"Just try it."

My power surged when I tapped into it and my body felt as if it was being ripped apart when I tried to focus it to do what I wanted. I couldn't even try directing it at him before my vision started to blur and I fell to my knees. I heard Gethin approach me and I held a hand out to stop him from getting closer.

"Oomph," he grunted and my vision cleared enough to see he'd shot clear across the training space, slamming into a wall.

"Sorry!"

"I think maybe we ought to take a break," he wheezed.

I wanted to offer him a hand up, but the magic within me was still too jazzed. I didn't trust that I wouldn't hurt him more. I left the training space and retreated back to my bedroom, pacing as I tried to dispel the energy that wound itself around my body still ready to strike.

Magic was supposed to be a natural part of me. It was supposed to obey my intent. So, why the fuck was I a live wire now? Downstairs, I caught the sound of voices and crept to the top of the stairs.

"You said she was powerful. But you didn't say she was so unpredictable," Gethin accused. "But it's like she's never cast a spell in her life. She's completely untrained. I've met five-year-olds with more control than her."

"We will make it work. We have to."

"I know you want her to be what you've been looking for ... but if she can't control her magic, there's no way anyone is going to follow her."

I didn't need to listen to this bullshit. I thundered down the stairs and left them both standing there, the front door slamming shut behind me. I didn't stop to think. I just ran.

SIX

The lake spread out in front of me and I turned right, running away from the cabin. My legs carried me along the bank as far and as fast as I could muster. I could feel the power within me begin to ebb as I ran, bleeding off the more I ran. Finally, I skidded to a halt and sunk to the grass, my legs collapsing. My heart hammered against my breastbone as my lungs fought for air. I bent over, taking steady breaths until my heart and lungs settled down a bit. I gazed up at the sky which was far more vivid blue than I'd ever seen in London and noticed for the first time there wasn't a cloud to be seen. The sun shone down unimpeded and it warmed my exposed skin.

Closing my eyes only conjured Aunt Nim's face.

There was so much I wanted to say to her. So much I *needed* to share, but I would never get the chance to now. I kept the tears at bay this time as I squatted there in the calm stillness of the forest by the lake. This was all so different from the life I'd lived until now.

I couldn't shake the disappointment in Gethin's words as he'd reported on my failed training session. It was one thing to believe I was a long-lost princess, and entirely another to have people expect me to be something I knew I wasn't. What hope did I have to earn the trust and respect of an entire kingdom if I couldn't keep it from someone who could rightly be called a fanboy?

Do you even want this?

The tiny voice in my head sounded so bloody judgmental. And yet, I couldn't dismiss the question. Yes, I had wanted a change from the life I'd been living. Though not because I'd hated all of it. I'd still wanted Aunt Nim in my life. I'd only wanted some independence. Not to lose everything I'd known my whole life.

High above me, a shadow drifted through the sky, but when I tried to find its origin, the sun blinded me. About thirty seconds later, something splashed in the center of the lake. I propped myself up on my elbows, hoping to catch a glimpse of whatever it was. All I could make out were massive ripples from its point of entry, reaching the shore closest to me. Whatever had made those ripples must have been massive as the water lapped at the bank not a foot from where I lay.

Maybe this wasn't the best spot to wallow if something or someone else was around. I stood up, wiping the grass off the backs of my legs and took a step in the direction I'd come. I stopped short though. I realized I had no sense of how far I was from Emerys' cabin nor did I have any confidence I could find my way back.

"Shit."

I turned back toward the lake in time to see new ripples forming a half meter from shore. I stood still, petrified of what might arise from the waters. Although, I did not expect to see a man's head emerge from the depths. In what felt like slow motion, the rest of his body followed: shoulders, biceps, and bare pectorals, then up to his hip bones. The closer he came the more I found myself staring. Water evaporated off his skin as soon as each body part met the morning air, leaving behind a vapor trail as he approached the shore.

To say I'd never seen someone so handsome as

him wasn't an exaggeration. His sharp jawline and the slender slope of his nose accentuated his intense dark gaze. The neat beard he sported made him appear almost regal. I didn't intend to look down and yet I chose the moment he stepped fully from the water to avert my gaze.

He was naked.

I swallowed the lump in my throat and was fairly certain I made a most impolite sound as he stood there in all his manly glory. I closed my eyes, but the image had seared into my memory.

"Do you mind?" he asked in a soothing baritone.

My eyes snapped open and I looked at him, taking care to focus only on his face. "Sorry?"

He gestured to a pile of clothing I'd been oblivious to lying on the grass. "Right."

I snatched up the shirt and tossed it at him, regretting the move instantly. Did he *really* need to cover up? He slid the lightweight fabric over his head and I held out the pants for him next. He shimmied into them without breaking eye contact with me.

"I didn't mean to disturb you," I said, finally finding the ability to form coherent sentences. "I just needed some air … I think I'm a bit lost."

"I don't usually take my morning swim with an

audience. But ... for a lady as beautiful as you, I think I can make an exception," he said with a smile. He tugged dark curls that hung just to his shoulders behind his ears, securing it in a low knot at the nape of his neck.

When he smiled, the expression lit up his whole face and I felt a warmth deep in my chest. I couldn't help glancing down at his waist as he stood there, waiting for ... what exactly?

"I would be happy to help reorient you if you could tell me where you were going."

"Oh. That's kind of you ..." I trailed off. I had hoped he'd fill in the pause with a name or a mobile number. *Do they even have mobile phones here?*

"Taron." He held out his hand.

My palm felt clammy as I extended it, feeling his firm hand wrap around mine. It was firm yet comforting like a reassuring embrace. I could picture those arms wrapping tight around me. *Fuck, why did he have to be wearing so many damn clothes?*

"This is generally the point in the conversation where you tell me your name."

"I ... I'm—"

"Morgan!" Gethin's voice filled the air and I turned to see him barreling toward us. He skittered in the grass. "I've been looking for you everywhere."

"Ah, she's yours, then?" Taron said with a smirk.

That was enough to break his hold on me. "I am owned by no one, thank you very much," I interjected.

"I just meant you are not as lost as you thought. You have an acquaintance to help you find where you're heading."

"Yes. She does." I caught the edge of bravado in Gethin's tone as he reached for my arm. "We need to be getting back."

Before I could point out just how useless he thought I was, he dragged me the way he'd come. I yanked my arm free of his grasp when the other man was a speck in the distance.

"I was just fine on my own. And you have terrible timing."

"Believe me, I was doing you a favor."

"You don't know the first thing about me," I snapped and stopped walking. "You have this idea in your head of how you think I'm supposed to be, but you don't actually know me."

He pivoted to face me. "How so?"

"If you'd bothered to ask me this morning, I would have told you my magic is utter shit. I've never been good at it. I'm not some great witch, come to do bloody anything. I'm not that person."

"You're right. I should have asked you instead of just assumed."

"What happened today, I have never felt that kind of power before. It was like I'd opened a tap and couldn't shut it off." I swallowed. "It was honestly a bit terrifying."

"And my telling Emerys how untrained you are didn't help anything." He took a step closer. "Morgan, I'm sorry. I've spent the better part of my life listening to Emerys talk about how one day, the rightful ruler would come home and take back what's hers. I think I dreamed up this person and … it hurts a little not to get the version I'd expected."

He began pacing. "But that's also not fair to you. Like you said, you didn't ask for any of this. It wasn't right for me to project my feelings onto you."

"I think I panicked a bit, too. My whole life, my Aunt Nim told me all these stories, like she knew one day I'd come back. But given how much I couldn't do in England; I think I psyched myself out of being able to do anything."

Gethin held his hand out to me. "How about we both agree we were wrong. We're going to need to work together to pull this off."

"I still have no bloody clue what we're doing, but sure … why not?" I shook his hand.

He led the way back to the cabin. I tried to make a mental map of how far we'd walked from the spot by the lake to the front door, but I still had no real reference points.

When we returned, Emerys stood waiting. She wore an expression of mixed disapproval and worry. She clearly didn't appreciate her pet project running off to parts unknown.

"You need to tell her what you told me," Gethin whispered in my ear. "About your magic. I think she can help."

"We should talk," I told her.

"Yes, we should." She raised her hands and nearby bushes reshaped themselves into a pair of benches.

I perched on the edge of one, not sure what to expect. What had initially appeared to be prickly and stubby branches wound themselves together tight enough to form a smooth surface. Just like the training space.

"Why did you run off?" Emerys spoke in a measured tone.

"Could you blame me? I'd just bolloxed up your little test exercise and Gethin called me useless. In case you hadn't realized it by now, I'm not the super witch you came looking for."

"I can see how that would have been upsetting."

"Gethin's already apologized. I guess we all came at this thing expecting different things. But I was also kind of freaked out. I've never felt this much power before and I don't know how to control it. I felt like I was drowning."

She brushed her hair over one shoulder and propped her elbows on her knees in a far more casual stance than I'd seen her adopt since meeting her the day before. "I hadn't considered bringing you home would unlock your power in that way."

I still didn't understand how she could know that my magic would act differently depending on where I was. She kept saying my magic was from here and not where I'd grown up. Although that didn't fully explain how she could predict the effect it had on me.

"We will work on it. I can't promise it is going to be easy, or enjoyable, but we will get your power in check."

"You two keep going on about some master plan you've hatched, but you haven't bothered to tell me about it. You said you'd answer my questions when we got here. Well, I think it's high time you clued me in."

"You're right. I do owe you answers." Emerys

straightened. "We are going to prove your claim to the throne. They are hosting a tournament of champions and Crown Prince, Arthur is participating."

"It's some overblown way to celebrate his coronation," Gethin added from the doorway.

"The point is those with strong magical talent are permitted to enter for the chance to face off against Arthur in the final round."

"So, he's guaranteed a spot?" I noted.

"Of course, he is," Gethin muttered.

"There is no question you possess enough raw magical talent to enter. We will just need to refine your skills. If we can do that, you would be able to compete."

"Let's say hypothetically all goes to plan. I get in and make it to this last round. How exactly is me beating him in some magic contest going to prove I'm the rightful heir, and not him."

"Because of Excalibur," Emerys replied in a deadpan.

"Like the mystical, all-powerful sword? Sorry, no. That sounds like utter nonsense."

"For generations, the Queen wielded Excalibur. It was a symbol not only of her right to rule, but the integrity of her bloodline. Each time an heir was born, a drop of their blood was shed on the blade, solidifying the bloodline's connection."

"Then Arthur came along, the first boy born in nearly a millennium, and all of a sudden not even Queen Ingrid could wield it. I obviously wasn't born yet, but from the stories I've heard around the pubs, it vanished and reappeared in the stone in the castle courtyard," Gethin explained.

"While I could not confirm it, I suspect Excalibur rejected Arthur's blood because he was not a true Pendragon and it has encased itself as a way to protect itself," Emerys added.

"And what, no one's tried to pull it out?" I quipped.

"Oh, Arthur has tried. And failed … many, many times," Emerys explained. "The official explanation is because he is a man, he has to prove his worth to wield the sword. I think most people expect he will do so during his final bout in the tournament. The show of strength in front of his subjects and neighboring dignitaries would cement his readiness to lead the kingdom."

"And you think I'd be able to pull it out? When someone who has probably trained his entire life for this moment can't do it?"

"When the time is right, I believe you will prove

your worth and be able to wield it, yes," Emerys answered.

I shook my head. "You've got a lot of faith in me."

"I have faith that now is the time to right a wrong I could not prevent thirty years ago. I will do whatever it takes to fix it." After a breath, she added, "And you would do well to have a little more faith in yourself. You were born for this, whether your experience to this point prepared you for it or not."

"Let's say I agree to this whole insane plan of yours. When do I have to apply?"

"The matches will be finalized tomorrow evening. You have until noon the same day to pass the entrance test."

I had to pick my jaw up from the ground. She couldn't possibly be serious. Even if I wasn't a walking disaster when it came to magic, preparing for some unknown entrance exam in less than a day was insanity.

"Do you know what the test is?"

"From what I have gleaned, it is different for each entrant."

Perfect.

"You better be a fucking miracle worker if you think twenty-four hours is going to make me good enough to control my magic and pass some unknown test that even you have no idea what it might be," I scoffed.

"You don't have to be perfect, just passable," Gethin offered with a wry grin and a wink.

"Helpful, mate. Real bloody helpful."

"I do not proclaim to be a miracle worker, but I have been around far longer than either of you and know a thing or two about harnessing magic. So, I suggest we get started," Emerys said with a determined nod.

SEVEN

Two hours later, all I'd managed to accomplish was cementing a divot in the dirt where my arse had landed for the millionth time. Emerys stood across the training space from me. I could see the frustration and the worry lines pinching the skin around her lips. She'd clearly not believed Gethin's assessment of my lack of ability.

"You must at least try," she chided as I hauled myself to my feet.

"I have been," I protested. "But I keep telling you, I can't control what comes out. I'm afraid it's going to drown me."

Emerys closed her eyes and took a deep breath. I watched her chest rise and fall until she reined in the emotion that threatened to spill out. She crossed the space and waved her hand. Behind me, the ground twisted and bent to form two small stools and I plunked myself down on one.

"I believe I have approached this the wrong way," Emerys admitted. "I heard your words, but did not understand your meaning."

"Just another reason why I'm a disappointment ..."

"You are not a disappointment." Emerys' tone was sharp and forceful.

I looked her in the eye. "Aren't I? I spent my whole life hearing stories of this fantastical place where I'm supposed to fit in. And the moment I get here, I can't even control my own magic. How am I supposed to be the hero you say I am if I can't even handle doing a simple spell?"

"If anything, you are a victim of circumstances beyond your control. We will sort this out."

"But how can you know that?"

"Because I have seen your greatness. As I told you yesterday, I have been looking for you for a long time. And I have known of your coming for far longer than that."

"Forgive me if I find that hard to believe."

Emerys stood and the stool receded back into the floor. She gestured for me to stand and follow her. I took my time getting to my feet. She made more hurrying gestures and I picked up the pace. She led me out of the cabin and back down the path we'd walked the day before. We passed the lake and heat washed over me at the image my mind conjured of Taron emerging from its depths.

"Come along," Emerys called ahead of me.

We picked our way through the brambles again, ending up back near the cave I'd spotted when we'd first made the transition from my world to this one. Emerys stepped up to the mouth of the cave and pressed her palm flat to the rocks worn smooth by time.

"This is the Crystal Cave," she said as if that should answer every question I had bouncing around in my head.

"Because ... it's full of crystals?" I surmised as we reached the back of the cave after only a dozen paces.

"You will find that this world's magic is far wilder than the one you left behind. It does not appear to need a mortal's whims to shape it constantly. I have found answers to many questions in this place. It was here that I first learned your existence and your importance."

She stepped inside, leaving me no choice but to follow. I stooped to avoid slamming my head into the tiny spirals of crystal hanging from the roof. Somehow, despite having no obvious light source or openings to let in natural light, the space was bathed in a soft pale glow. I could swear I heard a humming resonating off the walls and realized the crystalline structures must have been formed at just the right spots to harmonize within the cave.

Unlike when I'd stepped through the portal, the magic in this place felt calmer, more serene. I could sense the tension in my neck and shoulders loosen just by being in the cave.

What sort of magic was this?

"So, how exactly did a crystal show you I was meant to be this all important hero?"

Emerys pointed to a small outcropping of rocks near the back of the cave. Careful not to get my hair snagged in the stalactites above me. I shuffled to the outcropping to find a shallow pool of water. I couldn't see any source for the water and assumed it had been there for a while. In the back of my mind, I wondered why, if there was no source to refill the pool, it wasn't stagnant. The water was clear. I also recognized now was not the time to ask such questions.

We were here for a purpose—one I hoped would lead me to a way to control the surplus of power coursing through my veins before tomorrow morning. So, I perched on the edge of the rocks and peered into the still pool.

My reflection looked up at me, mirroring my position as one would expect. Then, I blinked and the water shifted, creating ripples on the surface to show me sitting on what I guessed was a throne, a crown set upon my head. I couldn't deny that the image filled some part of me that had been empty my entire life.

"So, it shows you what you want to see?"

"Sometimes. But it always shows you the truth," Emerys answered from behind me.

I peered down again, hoping the image would change to give me some hint of how I was meant to get to that point. "Couldn't it give me a hint of how I'm supposed to make this a reality?"

"It is up to you to find the path to it." I heard her footsteps crunch against the dirt of the cave floor as she closed the distance between us. She patted my arm and said, "But I think if you sit a while, it may illuminate your way."

With that, she turned and left me to sit in the cave in solitude. Her departure stopped me from pointing out that she was the one with all the magical knowledge that spanned ages, but she'd disappeared before I could even begin to form words. I turned to my reflection which had coalesced back into a mirror of my current position. Still, having seen that glimpse of what was waiting for me, I couldn't un-see it. It appeared I had no choice but to accept that at some point in the near future, I would reclaim something I never thought possible.

But only if I could get my damn magic under control.

I let out a sigh and addressed my reflection, "I don't suppose you've got any advice?"

The reflection of me sat up straighter and said, "You've just got to remember that you're the one in control, not the magic."

I sat there in stunned silence. I hadn't expected to get a response, let alone one that came back to me in my own voice. If I'd been anywhere else, I'd have chalked it up to too much working. My reflection still sat there, as if waiting for me to say something else.

"How do I turn my power down? It feels like I'm going to get swept away by it."

She held up her right hand in response and I could feel power ripple over me, as if her magic were mine. It was strong, but not overwhelming. "Picture it as an extension of your body, doing what you want it to do, not something that's happening to you."

I'd never thought of it that way. Maybe because until this point my magic had always felt so far away. I was hesitant to try anything within the cave's confines for fear of it backfiring. But my reflection gave me an encouraging smile.

Fuck, that's so weird.

As if sensing I needed something to react to, the tiny crystals overhead began to shake, threatening to come down on my head any second. The resonance that had until this moment been peaceful and soothing, shifted to something akin to a cat being skinned alive.

I swallowed back the lump in my throat and held my hands at shoulder height. As it had done earlier, my magic flooded every pore of my body.

"I'm in control," I said through gritted teeth and in my mind's eye I pictured a gauzy barrier between my head and the shards in the rock above me. The power within me leapt to attention, ready to race out of my body and do my bidding. "Not so much."

The scent of lime washed over me as my magic seeped out into the world and built a latticework of energy to keep the crystals from coming down. I did my best to commit to memory the way my magic felt as it responded in a more measured way to my desire. It cascaded from my core, up through my torso, through my shoulders, and past my elbows to become an extension of my fingertips as the inter-lacing energy wound itself tighter and tighter until it became a solid barrier.

I held my breath, waiting for it to collapse a moment later, but it remained solid and connected to me. *No more power.* I imagined myself throttling back the magic like easing off the gas pedal of a car and still the spell above me held.

I glanced down at my reflection in the pool and mirror Morgan gave me a smile and a wink. It couldn't have been that simple, could it? The cave shook around me and the impending danger receded. The resonance resolved into a more pleasant tone, as if to tell me it was safe to lower my barrier. I brought my arms back down to rest my hands in my lap and as I did so, I pictured the barrier turning into mist before dissipating completely. To my surprise, the barrier did just that overhead.

I straightened as much as the cave's cramped quarters would allow and made my way back toward the mouth of the cave where Emerys stood waiting. If she'd observed what I'd managed, she stayed mum.

"I trust your time within the Crystal Cave gave you clarity?"

"Not sure I'd call it clarity exactly, but I did manage to do something I didn't think possible," I answered. "I think I'm ready to try some proper training now."

"I am glad to hear you say that."

She started to lead the way back to the cabin and I fell into step beside her. "This is going to sound a bit off, but when you've gone in there has the pool, uh, talked back to you?"

She gave a knowing smirk. "Indeed, I have found myself in conversation with myself within its walls."

"I've never heard of magic being able to do that."

"As I've told you, the magic in this world is far wilder than what you've known. And there are more ways for it to express itself in this realm."

"Well, as long as you're not going to think I'm

mental for having a conversation with myself," I said.

"Sometimes it is our inner voice we need to hear from the most and it's also the hardest for us to find in the cacophony of the world around us," she offered as the cabin came back into view.

"Well, now that I've given myself a pep talk, let's see what I can really do."

EIGHT

Every muscle ached by the time the sky had turned to the velvety hues of night fall. We'd stopped briefly for food and drink sometime when the sun had begun its afternoon descent. Only sustenance hadn't felt that important now that I had a tentative grasp on my magic. The training room bore char marks and there were bits of wood splintered from where I'd tried to deflect Emerys and Gethin's attacks.

"It would really help to know what I was supposed to do to enter this tournament," I reminded them as I dragged myself to the table and Gethin set a cup of tea in front of me.

Gethin offered a supportive smile before he said, "The tournament entry is kept pretty secretive. I've heard people say that the test is tailored to each individual entrant's abilities. It's designed to show-case the best of what you can do."

"Sounds like you've got some experience," I noted.

He shook his head. "I've never made it past the qualifying round."

That did not fill me with confidence. I took a few sips of tea and made a vague gesture toward the training room. "I don't even know what I'm really capable of. But I can do damage to my surroundings. Does that count?"

"I think you will know what you must do when the time comes," Emerys said.

"Not to be a downer, but have you two thought about what happens if I don't make it into this tournament?"

I caught Gethin's jaw working as if to form words, but he stayed silent. I guessed he'd been about to offer up some version of 'that won't happen.' Except he thought better of it, given the day we'd had. I looked at Emerys expectantly.

"You may be untrained, but you have raw talent. And while it may not seem fair, you have something motivating you that the others do not—a destiny. I cannot believe the universe would bring you back to us only for you to fail."

"Relying on destiny seems a poor strategy," I muttered into my teacup.

I could see Emerys wanted to argue, but she kept quiet. Even I could sense we'd be going in pointless circles if the conversation carried on much more. If neither of them knew what awaited me in the morning, fine. I'd face whatever it was as best I could.

"Right, I'm going up to bed," I announced through a poorly stifled yawn.

In the back of my mind, I suspected Gethin had put something in my drink to help me sleep. Normally, I'd be offended by someone I barely knew trying to drug me, but honestly I could use all the help I could get. Somehow, I managed to make it up to bed before passing out.

I was back in the flat, standing at the sink with an empty coffee mug in my hand. It was Aunt Nim's favorite one. She'd bought it at a flea market when I was twelve. She'd said it reminded her of home. I accidentally dropped it a week later and we'd spent an afternoon gluing it back together. I'd stared at it for years and yet now, I couldn't quite remember what it looked like as I held it.

"It's funny how quickly memory fades, right?" Aunt Nim's voice caught me off guard.

I turned to find her standing there behind me. There was something off about the way she held her arms across her torso though. As if she was trying to keep something in—blood. The agony of losing her hit me all over again and the mug slipped from my fingers into the sink, shattering into a dozen pieces.

"I'm so sorry I couldn't save you," I said through shallow gasps.

"No tears, my beautiful girl. You're where you're meant to be now," Aunt Nim replied, her cheeks turning paler by the second.

Our surroundings shifted from the flat to the sprawling forest just beyond Emerys' cabin. I could make out the silhouette of Camelot's castle in the distance.

"We were so close to the portal, a plane ride away all these years. Why didn't you ever bring me back yourself?" I dried my eyes with the back of my hand.

"Selfishness. I knew what awaited me here if I ever returned. I'd defied a direct order from my King and I knew I'd pay for it with my life one day. But I knew I couldn't harm you, my brave girl."

"I don't feel brave. I don't feel like I'm meant for any of this. It would be so much easier if you were here with me."

She stepped up and pressed a hand to my cheek. I could feel the warmth fading from her skin. "You are never alone, Morgan. I may be gone, but the things I've taught you live on in you. Trust in those sent to teach you. And when the time is right, you will do what I never could."

"What's that?"

"Fight ... Fight for this place, for the people in it. You'll find your place. You'll find your people."

Some part of me knew this wasn't real, but I couldn't resist pulling her to me in one final embrace. I kissed her cheek and held her until she faded, leaving me standing in a place that felt so very far from home.

I woke to the quiet stillness of my bedroom in Emerys' cabin. I half-expected Gethin to come knocking to rouse me, but the second floor was silent as I climbed out of bed and headed for the loo. I grabbed a quick shower and headed down to the kitchen. I found the coffee pot and filled it, waiting for the ground beans to percolate. Leaning against the sink I was reminded of my dream. I could almost feel Aunt Nim's body against mine and I held back tears.

"Get it together," I chided myself as the coffee finished brewing. I rummaged in the cabinets until I found a thermos and filled it to the top. I had no idea how long it would take us to get to the tournament grounds. Except Emerys' statement about entries closing at noon stuck out in the back of my mind. My phone said it was only 6:30 a.m.

I left the cabin behind, tracing the path I'd taken the day before, sipping my coffee as I went. The lake came into view and I scanned the surface, hoping to see evidence of Taron. I made it a quarter of the way along the lakeshore before I spotted a pile of clothing on the grass.

This time, when he emerged from the water, I wasn't so caught off guard. But that didn't mean I missed sneaking a little peek as the water sizzled against his dark skin. He spotted me as he tugged his pants on first.

"Twice in two days, is this going to become a habit?" he called, leaving his shirt on the grass. "Morgan, was it?"

"Yes. And I'm just on a walk, enjoying my coffee. I can't help if that walk happened to take me by your favorite skinny-dipping spot."

He laughed and the early morning sunlight sparkled in his eyes, turning his irises almost bronze. "So, what you're saying is I should get used to having an audience?"

Every retort I could think of died on my lips. I could suggest he find somewhere else to swim or put on a swim suit. My libido rejected both ideas vehemently. "I suppose you should."

He finally tugged on his shirt. "What really brings you out here this early?"

I could lie to him. But what would be the point in that? "Just trying to clear my head. I'm entering the tournament they're holding for the Crown Prince. I'm a bit nervous."

"Ah yes, Camelot's golden boy."

"Not a fan?"

"Don't let him hear me say this, but I've always thought him a bit too entitled. You know the whole first boy born in nearly a millennium and all that."

"I have heard that," I agreed. "I also heard that he's the one to face in the final bout if someone were to make it that far."

"I'm sure you'll do well," he said.

"Everyone keeps saying that. I'll believe it when it actually happens."

"Manifest it. Put it out into the world and let the world reward you."

"Thanks. I'll give it a try."

"Guess I'll see you tomorrow," he said and offered a small bow before starting off along the lakeshore away from me.

By the time I made it back to the cabin, the rest of its occupants were bustling about. Gethin set a platter of fresh pastries on the table along with just squeezed juice. I tucked in, setting the thermos on the table beside me.

"So, how long is it going to take to get there?" I asked in between bites.

"An hour," Emerys answered. "We have a twenty-minute walk to the nearest transit."

"Please tell me it's not a horse and buggy," I quipped.

Emerys arched a brow at my words. "I do not know what you have heard but Camelot has come happily into the modern age."

"We've had high speed rail lines for ages," Gethin added.

"Great."

THE RAIL CAR was sparsely populated when we boarded. I watched as we hurtled toward the heart of Camelot. The serenity of nature gave way to a sprawling metropolitan infrastructure and modern convenience. It was like stepping into yet another new world. Only one appeared more familiar than where I'd spent the last forty-eight hours. The train eased to a stop far gentler than any train on the London Underground ever could.

I trailed Emerys and Gethin as they disembarked and headed through a set of metal turnstiles into the heart of the city proper. The castle loomed large ahead of us as we maneuvered through the crowd waiting in queues for tournament tickets. There was a roped off area labeled, 'Entrants Only.' Emerys and Gethin stopped short of entering.

"We cannot go in with you, not until you are a confirmed contender. Then you are allowed an entourage," Emerys explained. She gestured to a grey-haired woman seated at a table just beyond the barrier. "She will ensure you are administered the qualifying round."

I didn't like not having them with me, but I could understand the reason. Only allowing potential participants in would presumably cut down on the amount of cheating. I stepped around the rope and approached the woman. She glanced up at me and said, "Name?"

"Morgan le Fey."

She cast a sideways look toward where Emerys and Gethin stood watching. After a beat, she scribbled something on her clipboard and locked gazes with me. "I'm glad you were able to make it in time."

"So ... uh, what do I have to do exactly?"

"What category are you entering under?"

There's categories?

"I, uh ... I'm not really sure."

She gave me a pitiful look. "Are you witch, fae, or dragon?"

"Oh. Witch."

She held out what looked like a biometric reader and gestured for me to place my right hand on it. I did so without argument or question, and only winced slightly when the device zapped me. The scent of limes tickled the back of my nose.

"Good on you for not lying," the woman said before pointing toward a small tent. "Good luck. For what it's worth, I hope you make it through."

"Thanks."

You can do this. You are a witch damn it ... and according to everyone a powerful one at that.

The moment I stepped into the tent the world tilted off its axis. The space was far larger than it had any right to be. The air crackled with energy and power. I could feel it calling to my magic, begging it to respond.

"Your objective is simple," an alto voice boomed from overhead. "You must face three obstacles. Complete fewer than two and you will be eliminated from entry."

"Okay, only have to survive two. That's not so bad," I told myself out loud.

The tent filled with thick fog, blinding me instantly. I couldn't see my hand six inches in front of my face. Panic gripped me for a moment before I heard Aunt Nim's voice in the back of my head.

"Fog's worst enemy is light. Be the beacon in the dark my pretty girl."

She'd told me that on particularly stormy nights as a child. We'd always lit a candle and her magic had sustained it through the morning until the sun could come out and dispel the fog.

I could hear vague noises that could have been someone or something else in the space around me. They grew closer, the shuffling footfalls growing louder from my left. My basic sense of self-preservation kicked in. I held my left hand aloft and pictured it shining bright as the sun. An electrical current of magic bolted up my arm, leaving my elbow tingling as a thousand limes let loose their citrus scent and my hand blazed an iridescent green. I swiped the light in the direction of whatever was approaching to reveal some creepy wraith-like creature. It flinched as the light touched it and I charged at it, chasing it out of existence.

The fog dissipated some around me, affording me a small field of vision. There was no indication whether I'd passed the first obstacle, but I assumed I had. I moved forward in the direction I thought had been in front of me when I'd entered the tent. I took a step to my right and heard something click beneath my shoe.

My mind immediately filled with the sound of ticking as I tried to bend, using the light from my hand to reveal what I'd stepped on. It certainly looked like a land mine. But they wouldn't really attempt to blow up their entrants, would they? Still, I couldn't make myself move from the spot.

The ticking grew louder and I realized it wasn't in my head after all. Whatever I was standing on was counting down. I didn't have the luxury of just standing around, hoping some knight would come along and rescue me.

"Think, Morgan." I muttered under my breath.

I'd watched enough action films to know that if I could get something of equal weight to my body mass onto the mine, it might not trigger. Or it would give me enough time to get clear of the blast. But the fog still obscured everything beyond the radius of my magical light. Even if I could find something, I'd need both hands to maneuver it into place. Yet if I let the light go, I'd be blind again.

I closed my eyes, taking a slow inhale. I had seen Aunt Nim multitask with magic tons of times. It looked as if it were as easy to her as breathing. I'd never asked her how she'd managed it. Why bother when I couldn't even manage a single spell reliably? But it had to be doable.

"Here goes nothing."

Keep the light going.

I put my intent out into the world and flicked my left hand upward, as if to let go of the light. When I opened my eyes, the light hovered above me, casting its greenish glow from overhead. It dispelled enough of the fog to reveal the ground was made of soil and small shrubs. I could work with that. I'd watched Emerys bend the nature around her to her will over the last two days.

I reached out with both hands, careful not to shift my weight and tried to sculpt a human-like shape from the nearby shrubs, uprooting them to make a torso and limbs. It wasn't perfect by any means, but it would have to do.

"Sorry about this," I said, addressing the shrub mannequin as I raised my arms and watched it levitate into position just beside me. I took a deep breath and stepped off the mine. The shrub figure landed in my place and I threw myself into a roll. Ten seconds later, the shrub mannequin exploded in a shower of branches, roots, and greenery.

I had told Gethin I was good at damaging my surroundings. The blast's shockwave rippled over me and sent me rolling about half a meter away from where I'd been standing. In the chaos, my concentration slipped and the fog pressed in around me again.

I beat back my fear as I crawled forward in the direction I'd been going the whole time. Somewhere above me, something let out a guttural roar and I froze in place. *Shit, what was that?* I hastily raised my hand, casting a much feebler light this time. It was still enough to reveal the underside of something scaly and *massive*. What had the woman asked me? What category I was? She'd mentioned dragons. Surely one of those wouldn't be small enough to fit inside this tent.

Nothing from Aunt Nim's magical lessons from

my childhood came to mind. We'd never discussed dragons. I recalled that I had thought it strange there weren't any in her tales, but I'd never questioned it. There was no way I was going to be able to defeat a dragon.

I could hear its wings beating and felt a shift in the air currents above me. It was enough to give me a clear view, however brief, of the exit. It was maybe a meter and a half away. If I could get to my feet, I might be able to make a break for it and pray I made it without getting cooked.

"Complete fewer than two and you will be eliminated," the woman's voice echoed in my head.

I had to hope that I'd done enough to pass the first two obstacles. As I got into a runner's stance, I let out a little more power. *Make me fast.*

My legs pumped and I hurtled toward the exit. Above me the dragon roared, but it never attacked. Maybe I'd misjudged the obstacle, but I didn't have time to consider it more. I ran until the fog vanished and I found myself standing at the tent flap I'd first entered.

Disorientation hit me like a ton of bricks and I staggered to the side, groping for something solid to steady me. I spotted Emerys and Gethin waiting where I'd left them. How long had it been? It felt like ages had passed since I'd gone inside. Somehow, I recalled entering the tent not long after 10:00 a.m. The clock sitting on the table by the woman who'd checked me in now read 10:22 a.m. Twenty minutes at most?

"Congratulations, you have qualified for the Tournament of Champions," the alto voice announced.

Bloody brilliant. Now I just had to hope the rest of this thing wasn't nearly as deadly.

The woman who'd checked me in, offered me a small lapel pin. "Wear this during the tournament. So long as you're on the board, it will identify you as a participant."

I affixed the pin—a small silver shield with two swords crossed over it—to the collar of my shirt. After that I followed Emerys and Gethin away from the entrant qualifying tent. People were still queued to purchase their tickets and a few spotted the pin. They pointed and whispered behind their hands. I offered a hesitant wave before I felt a tug on my arm.

Emerys led me toward a different roped off area labeled, 'Participants' and ushered me forward. In my peripheral vision I caught her head swiveling from side to side, as if searching for someone. No, not searching, making sure she wasn't spotted.

"When you said you had a falling out with the Queen, you weren't like banned from castle grounds were you?" I asked in a stage whisper as we fell in line behind a few other people sporting pins. Some of them bore the same insignia as my own. Others were more ornate and gilded, but still considered similar in design.

"Last I heard, she had not issued any orders to remove me from the grounds. But I admit, I have not been to the castle in some time. Given our differences and the importance of this year's tournament, I would not put it past her to have heightened security," she answered in a long breath.

My own anxiety sprang to the forefront of my mind and I couldn't' help looking around at the throngs of people, too. It struck me just how foreign I truly was in this place. I might have been born in this world, but with the exception of the two people standing beside me, I knew no one. Not really even them. How well did I really know my companions?

"If you can't stay, she's got me," Gethin said cheerily. "And if nothing else, I'll make sure she's had a proper meal before each round."

"Let's not panic just yet," Emerys said, but I could tell even she didn't believe her words.

"I suppose you owe me an I told you so," I said as the line progressed.

"What were your obstacles?" Gethin asked, ignoring my statement.

"Creepy fog monsters and a landmine. Oh, and a dragon. I'm pretty sure I failed the last bit with the dragon. I just ran as fast as I could to get out. Didn't even engage."

"Not to sound ignorant, but what's a landmine?"

I eyed him skeptically. "A device you put in the ground that explodes to take out your enemy. Usually triggered by pressure and shifting weight."

"Is it magical?"

"Not particularly. Pretty mundane actually," I answered.

"Sorry, just never heard of something so … nonmagical being in the trials."

"Aunt Nim loved watching action movies. I've seen enough to know you need to replace the exact weight. It gives you enough time to roll clear or keeps it from triggering altogether."

"And how'd you defeat the fog?"

"Magical light. We had some nasty fog growing up and my Aunt Nim would always light a candle, infused with a little magic to keep it burning to dispel the darkness."

"Seems like she prepared you better than you thought," Emerys noted softly.

"Yeah. I guess she did."

"I never got to fight a dragon when I had taken on the qualifying trial. Then again, I never actually made it through," Gethin said with a pout.

"Just hope I won't have to face a real one."

"Statistically, it's probable one of your rounds would pit you against one," Gethin answered.

"Not helpful, mate."

"I'm just trying to temper your expectations."

"How about you tell me what this whole thing is even supposed to be?"

The line ahead of us moved forward to reveal a large complex that looked like a hotel with rooms on three of the four walls. Gethin tapped my shoulder and hooked his thumb over his shoulder. I turned to see a massive screen displaying the tournament bracket—four rounds split in two brackets set to meet in the middle. I spotted Arthur's name already on the top of the left bracket. I pitied whoever faced him on his way to the finals match. There was no chance he wouldn't make it there. The righthand bracket was slowly populating as well.

"Each round you've got to get four points to advance to the next round. They usually space the rounds out every other day. So, the top bracket goes tomorrow, and then bottom bracket the day after. It usually takes about two weeks to complete the tournament."

"Maybe by then I'll actually be decent?" I mused.

"Participants are expected to remain on tournament grounds when they are competing," Emerys said as we neared a central table with what appeared to be room assignments.

"I was just getting used to the cabin," I said. But I didn't mention it meant missing my morning encounters by the lake with Taron.

"Lucky for you, I know a few secret passages," she whispered before ducking her head and falling into step behind me. She gave me a nudge between the shoulder blades.

The entrant ahead of me had finished at the table and I was left standing there awkwardly. A rotund man with bushy eyebrows looked up from a clipboard not unlike the one the woman had possessed at the qualifying area.

"Name?" he asked in a lilting accent.

"Morgan le Fey," I answered on autopilot.

He poured over his clipboard, squinted at the

bottom, and then looked up at me. "Late entrant I see." He gathered a pile of papers with two key cards and held them out to me. "You're entitled to have one member of your team with you in the lodging area. You can have two members on the grounds during tournament rounds. Fill out these forms and leave them on the outside of your door when you're finished."

I took the papers, but didn't move. "Aren't I supposed to find out where I'm meant to go next?"

He pointed to the papers. "Room assignment is in there. Final bracket determinations will be made this afternoon. We will be holding the opening cere-mony at sunset." He gave me a small smile. "Don't worry, you won't miss where to go."

Before I could ask about sharing rooms with other entrants, I felt someone tug me out of line by the elbow. I glanced over my shoulder to find Gethin leading me away from the queue of people still getting their room assignments.

"Let's see where we've ended up," he said, taking the papers from me.

I scanned the crowd, realizing I'd lost sight of Emerys. But maybe it was by design. As soon as she'd gotten within the castle's confines with people she didn't feel she could trust, she'd done her best to obscure her identity. Part of me wondered if she'd really been away for three decades, were there many people who would recognize her on sight?

"We're east wing," Gethin said, drawing my focus back to him.

"We're not meant to room with other entrants, right?" I whispered as I followed him to a staircase that led up to the second level rooms.

"From what I'm reading here … no, we room by ourselves. Less chances of spying and cheating."

He stopped walking halfway down the balcony connecting the upper set of rooms at a door marked, E14. He held one of the key cards up to the locking mechanism and it clicked, swinging open. Everyone else must have qualified earlier, because I could see small clusters of people scattered around the grounds below.

"Let's get the boring stuff done first and then we can scope out the competition," Gethin called.

"You're going to be the annoying bloke who insists on living vicariously through me, aren't you, Fanboy?" I pulled the door shut behind us.

"Let me have this, Morgan. I've been waiting my entire life for something like this," he said and rifled through the papers.

I took a minute to acclimate to our surroundings. The room was spacious, sporting two queen size beds. I couldn't deny I was grateful we wouldn't be sharing a bed. I walked past Gethin and ducked into the loo. There was a full size shower, a simple sink, and a vanity on the opposite wall of the toilet.

"Has this place always been around or did they construct it for this tournament?" I called as I poked around the closet.

"They built it about forty years ago. Thanks to magic, it renovates itself to keep up with the times."

I moved back to the main room. "So, what are these forms I'm meant to be filling out?'

"Standard stuff. Medical releases, agreeing you won't sue the crown if you're injured and your estate won't go after them if you're killed."

A strained sound passed my lips. "Please tell me that was a poorly delivered joke."

He looked at me, a serious expression on his face. The glasses only made him look sterner. "No joke. These tournaments can get dangerous. I mean there are limits, but the rules are pretty liberal in what kinds of magic you can use."

"Before I sign anything, I need to know exactly what I'm getting into," I said, crossing my arms over my chest and sitting down on the nearest bed.

The sternness faded into something more akin to worry and almost a whine. "You can't back out."

"Pretty sure so long as I haven't signed anything, I can back out." I didn't tell him that I was still questioning whether it was even worth it to go through with this. I wouldn't cheat and there was no guarantee I'd make it to the final round against Arthur.

"You're right though. How can we expect you to jump into something you know nothing about? The tournament is pretty straightforward. There's four rounds in two brackets."

"I figured that much out from the giant bracket board outside," I said in a deadpan.

He rubbed at the nape of his neck in embarrassment. "Right. Uh ... well, in order to advance to the next round, you've got to earn four points. You need three hits to get a point. And you have to win by at least one point."

I considered the basic rules. When he explained it that way, it appeared rather straightforward. "Sounds a bit like tennis. Is it just the one set of four or is it a best two out of three or whatever?"

"Just the one round," he answered after a moment.

"And how do you get a hit? Sounds violent."

"It can be. Each entrant wears a special uniform.

If you get hit in certain places, it will light up and count as a point."

"And anything goes magic wise?"

"I mean you can't outright murder anyone, but wounding them isn't against the rules."

"Let me guess, some ego-obsessed man decided this blood sport was a fun way to spend an afternoon," I grumbled, but took the papers from Gethin's hands and read over them.

"You know, I'm not actually sure where the tournament's rules originated." I could see the look in his eyes, a longing to go digging for answers.

"I'll sign the bloody forms, but if I die, I'm going to find a way to come back from the dead and haunt you," I threatened and scribbled my signature on the pages before attaching them to the plastic collection bin on the outside of the door.

"I know you're nervous and you're worried you don't belong here, but you do. If things hadn't gone wrong all those years ago, we'd be getting ready to celebrate your coronation, not his," Gethin said in a soft tone. "But we'll set things right. I know we will."

"I'm just going to look around," I said and stepped onto the balcony. More people milled about on the ground level than when we'd first entered the room. Everyone *looked* human, but I knew better. I tried to look at ear shapes, but most of the women had their ears covered by their hair and the men wore sports bands. I was so lost in my observations I didn't hear the footsteps approaching from my right until the floorboards beside me groaned with added weight. I caught a figure out of the corner of my eye and my heart jumped into my throat.

A slender, handsome man with dirty blond hair, clear blue eyes, and a neatly trimmed beard stared at me. I immediately disliked him. It was like he was purposely oozing charm in the hopes of distracting me from whatever had brought him up here.

"Can I help you?" I croaked out.

"I've met all of the entrants for the tournament, but I don't' recognize you." He pointed to the pin on my collar. "And I know everyone from Camelot."

That appeared unlikely. "I'm a late applicant," I answered. I caught sight of the pin on his own lapel. It was more ornate than mine and included a bit of scrollwork along the bottom with a motto I couldn't quite make out.

"Well, late applicant, as the reigning champion, and crown prince, allow me to welcome you to the tournament and wish you the best of luck."

The bottom dropped out of my stomach as his

words hit me. The man I hoped to dethrone was standing in front of me, none the wiser of my identity. "Bet you say that to everyone," I blurted.

"I do. It's part of the pomp and ceremony of it all."

"Well, I hope you don't expect to win just because you're the golden boy," I said, instantly regretting the taunt in my words.

He let out a small laugh. "Oh, no. It wouldn't be much fun if they weren't honest matches. I'll see you around ..." he glanced at the paperwork on the door behind us. "Morgan."

He sauntered down the balcony past the other rooms just as the door behind me opened and Gethin walked out.

"What was that about?"

"Pomp and ceremony," I answered. "If the royal family didn't know I was here before, they sure as hell do now."

Let the fun begin.

I did my best to wipe Arthur's smug face from my mind as Gethin and I settled into the room and waited for the opening ceremony. I reached for my phone on instinct, wanting to call Jules and fill her in on the insanity that had become my life. But there was no recognizable signal for the phone to pick up on. The only person besides Aunt Nim I wanted to share this with would never know I was finally fulfilling the destiny we'd envisioned as children.

"If you're worried about Arthur, don't be. Just focus on getting through one round at a time," Gethin offered in an attempt to read my state of mind as I paced.

"I'd actually managed to put him out of my mind until now. I'm just feeling a bit out of sorts. My best mate back home would love all of this. If I'm honest, she believed in the whole Camelot and lost princess thing more than I ever did. It feels weird to be here without her."

His face fell. "I'm sorry. That's got to feel so isolating and lonely."

"It's not what I was hoping for right before this big fight, but it's not like I can just pop back and pick her up." A thought occurred to me and excitement welled in my chest. "Or can I?"

"Afraid not. The portal doesn't work that way. From what I've read it is only active when there's a reason. Usually on a world-changing scale."

"Damn it."

"I'm probably a poor substitute for your friend, but what can I do to help?"

"I need you to be my eyes and ears on the grounds. When we find out who I'm going up against first, I'm going to need all the information I can get about them."

"I think I can handle that. From the stories I've heard they don't pay much attention to the entourage. Everyone is so focused on the entrants themselves."

"For someone who's never actually been in the

tournament, you know an awful lot about how it runs," I quipped.

"I know people," he retorted with a smirk. "Now come on, let's get ready for the ceremony."

As if on cue, two sharp knocks sounded on the door. I opened it find a woman with a long, thin face standing across the threshold with a uniform draped over her arm.

"The Opening Ceremony starts in twenty minutes. Be down in the entrant's tent in ten minutes for the procession." She foisted the uniform at me and marched down the balcony toward the stairs.

I studied the uniform as I stepped back into the room. It was sleek and black with patches of harder material sewn into the shoulders, chest, and thighs. I flipped it over and found the same material.

"Those parts are what register hits," Gethin explained.

"Right. This is so bloody strange,' I muttered and ducked into the loo to change.

I'd expected it to be ill-fitting and constricting. Surprisingly it was breathable and hugged my body, but it wasn't skin-tight. I still had a good range of motion.

"Look at you," Gethin beamed as he transferred

my pin to the lapel of the uniform. "Come on, you don't want to be late."

Minutes later, I found myself standing amongst a group of fifteen other people all dressed in identical uniforms. Arthur stood out amongst the group as the other entrants gave him a wide berth. Up close, I could see that most of the pins weren't as ornate as I'd thought. Most people in the group appeared to gravitate toward those with the same crest though.

"May I have your attention," the man who'd given me my room assignment called. "I will have those representing Camelot here, then those for the Dragon court behind, and those from the Seelie territories at the end."

I shuffled into place amongst four other people with Camelot's pins. Five people sporting the dragon crest settled into the line behind me, and another five took up the tail end. That left Arthur to lead the procession. I caught him securing his crown before leaving the tent.

Our procession wove through the participant lodgings and out onto the castle grounds where stadium seating had already been erected. Spectators filled the seats as we moved through a small entryway and stopped in front of a dais where a woman sat on a throne. The simple circlet crown on her head was enough of a clue as to her identity. The queen. My mother. She wore an elegant knee-length tunic in vibrant blue over grey leggings. A larger version of the pin I'd been given sat affixed to her collar. Hers also bore a decorative ribbon design and a motto: *Materna magica*.

She scanned the entrants and when our gazes met I felt a jolt in my stomach. Would she somehow recognize me as her own flesh and blood? There was no hint of recognition in her eyes as she looked on to the person behind me. It wasn't exactly like looking in a mirror, but I got a hint at what I might look like in another thirty years. It was stupid of me to think she'd somehow know me just by looking at me. That was a little girl's wish and something I'd given up on ages ago.

The crowd in the stadium cheered as we stood on display. I did my best not to squirm under their collective attention. Behind me, I heard weight shift and a large screen projected what was going on behind me. The queen stood and approached a raised podium with a microphone. I braced for the echo of feedback from standing so close to her, but it never came.

"Citizens of Camelot, honored guests and

entrants, I would like to welcome you all to this year's Tournament of Champions." She beamed at the assembled crowd and I could see real excitement in her features. I couldn't help studying the way her eyes crinkled in the corners when she smiled. I could see myself in her expression.

She pivoted a quarter turn to address the right hand side of the stadium. "As a country, we look forward to this gathering each year as it brings our people together in a common bond of healthy competition and fun. This year is particularly special as we will not only crown a winner at the week's end, but my son, Arthur, will take his rightful place as King of Camelot."

Whoops, cheers, and whistles went up from the crowd. I spotted several rows of men who looked to be in their thirties sporting shirts spelling out Arthur's name across their chests. I also caught Arthur raise a hand to acknowledge his ardent supporters on the big screen. He opened his mouth as if to speak, but the queen cut him off. At least temporarily.

"As is tradition, the previous year's winner will light the ceremony beacon."

Arthur left the line of entrants and joined the queen on stage. I hadn't noticed the beacon until now, perched on a silver pedestal. I noted a small placard at the bottom with Arthur's name etched onto it. It must have doubled as the tournament trophy. Shaped almost like a champagne glass fashioned out of crystal and sapphires, there was a small central spot that looked like it might have once held the wick of a candle.

With a flourish and wave of his hand, Arthur lit the beacon. The flame he produced leapt high into the air, shimmering a vibrant blue before settling back into a normal yellow-orange glow.

"Let the tournament commence." Arthur's voice boomed throughout the stadium.

The crowd cheered again and the image on the screen shifted, replaced by the bracket board I'd seen in the entrants' lodgings. Arthur's name remained on the top left bracket, facing off against someone named Merril Farnaz. My eyes glazed over the other names in the search for my own. There, at the bottom right bracket sat my name. I faced off against someone called Shunae DeVoe.

Arthur returned to his spot in line and led our procession out of the stadium to raucous applause. We marched back to our lodgings and I scanned the waiting faces for Gethin or Emerys. The stoic faces around me melted away once we were out of range of the public. The five entrants sporting the dragon crest shuffled off together, as did the fae.

"There you are," Gethin called from behind me.

I spun, resisting the urge to throw my arms around him at seeing his familiar face. Before I could open my mouth to respond, he continued on, "We need to go study."

"Study? This is a tournament, not a quiz," I reminded him.

"You're facing Shunae DeVoe," he said, as if I hadn't been able to read the bracket.

"So I saw." It was then I registered the mild panic in his tone. "Why does that freak you out?"

He gave a nervous laugh. "Oh, she's only last year's runner up. And ... uh, she's brutal."

BY SOME MIRACLE, my round wasn't scheduled until two days from the opening ceremony. It gave Gethin and I plenty of time to hunker down in my room and study all of the available footage of Shunae's previous matchups. Each one filled me with a deeper sense of dread as the day wore on. I didn't sleep that night at all. Every time I closed my eyes, I saw her coming for me.

"I'm going to die," I announced after watching the sixth video of her slamming someone into a wall with just a wave of her hand.

"This is good, actually," Gethin said when a knock came at the door on Sunday morning, a mere two hours before my match was set to begin.

"You're mental," I noted as he opened the door to reveal Emerys in a hooded cloak, as if she'd stepped out of a medieval history book. If she was trying to be inconspicuous, she was doing a piss poor job of it.

"I trust you have had some time to learn your opponent's fighting style?" Emerys slid her cloak off and slung it casually over the back of a chair.

"If by fighting style you mean the way she just throws people around like rag dolls. Then sure, I've studied it. Your apprentice here thinks this is wonderful."

"I didn't say wonderful. I said it's good. You get past her in round one and people are going to start to take notice of you. Everyone knows she was runner up last year."

"Gethin isn't wrong. Making it through your first match against such a strong opponent would make you a viable contender for the final fight."

"How am I supposed to fight someone like that?

Let alone last long enough to score ... what ... four points?"

"Haven't you been watching?" Gethin scoffed.

"Yeah. All I've seen are people getting decimated by her."

"But she didn't win. And it wasn't even a close match last year. Arthur won by two points. I'm not convinced he didn't let her get a few hits in just for fun, for the showmanship of it all." Gethin waved back to the screen. "Here, watch."

I let out a groan, but joined him as he hit 'Play' on the screen. He'd slowed it down to half speed and I followed his finger as he pointed out how Arthur got behind her and had managed to hit her from behind. Unlike in the sports I was used to—not that I was conceding this was a sport—he was permitted to hit her as many times as he wanted. It's how he'd gained points so quickly.

"So, you're telling me I've just got to dodge and pray I can hit her fast enough to get points?"

"You won't know until you try," Gethin said. "And she favors her right hand. If you can find a way to restrain that hand, you've got a shot at getting her into a vulnerable position."

"You may not feel it, but you are more evenly matched than you believe," Emerys said. "You are both witches. You draw your power from the same elements. Use that to your advantage."

"I'm just going to remind you that no one's going to want someone who gets pummeled near to death as their leader."

"You should get changed," Emerys said, ignoring my doom and gloom attitude.

I retreated to the loo and donned my tournament uniform. Just like two days ago, it fit snuggly without restricting my movement. The silver pin on my lapel shone in the overhead light. I couldn't help but run my finger across the two crossed swords and the tiny shield beneath them.

"Well, Aunt Nim ... Here I am, just where you said I'd one day be. Wish you could have warned me about this blood sport tournament. I just have to trust you prepared me for what's coming," I whispered to my reflection.

"Morgan, the attendants have come to bring you down to the arena," Gethin called.

I twisted my hair into a knot at the nape of my neck and joined them on the balcony. Emerys fell into step behind Gethin and I with her head looking down. I kept my mouth shut as we left the lodging area and passed through the heart of the castle's courtyard. I spotted workers moving about the space, setting up stadium seating.

"The final round is held in the courtyard," Gethin explained when I gave him a confused look.

We passed by the large stone where a sword sat lodged within from halfway up the blade. The sapphires on its hilt glistened in the morning sunlight and I felt my heart skip a beat. Blood rushed in my ears and I felt my body jerk to the left, as if drawn to the weapon by some unseen force.

Free me.

It was like it knew I was here and it knew who I really was. Gethin put a firm hand on my arm and guided me back into formation. If I'd doubted the truth of who I was before, a part of me couldn't help but believe it now.

Once the stone and sword were out of my line of sight, the strange feeling receded. Instead, my adrenaline spiked as we stepped into the arena. I could see a large divider midway through the stadium.

"The second match starts this afternoon," Gethin explained, as if reading my mind.

"What if we haven't finished yet?"

"That's why there's a divider." He patted my arm. "You've got this, Morgan."

With a firm shove between the shoulder blades, he sent me staggering forward. I stepped beside Shunae, who didn't bother acknowledging my existence. That is until the referee approached us.

"I want a clean match today, ladies. I will not be cleaning up blood. Am I clear?"

"Yes, Sir," I answered.

"Understood," Shunae replied in a deep alto voice.

"Follow me out to the pitch," the referee said.

Shunae stepped in front of me; leaving me no choice but to bring up the rear in our little processional. The crowd cheered upon seeing Shunae. She gave them all a confident fist pump before taking her position on the far side of the arena.

The referee blew two loud bursts on what looked like a trumpet and shouted, "Begin!"

ELEVEN

Every muscle in my body froze as the referee's words rang in my ears. The thousands of eyes watching us from the stands were a palpable weight pressing in on me. The sudden realization that I didn't know what the fuck I was doing made everything take on an angry red haze. Every doubt raced through my head like a screaming freight train. I wasn't some champion. No, I was a bartender from London with shitty magic. I wasn't a savior. I was no one, a nobody. This was a huge mistake.

My fear and indecision gave Shunae an easy opening to make the first move. One minute she stood on the other side of the pitch, and the next she was springing into the air toward me like a predator about to pounce. I had just enough time to register the movement before she tackled me to the ground. My head slammed against the grass with a painful 'thud' and pain erupted behind my eyes.

"Get off," I grunted, trying to swat at her as she pressed the full weight of her body against my torso.

Above me, she just bared her teeth and waved her hands like she was tying a knot. "I don't know who you are, new girl, but you're not going to beat me."

Air rippled around me as I felt her magic spring to life and settle over me. She rolled off me and I was about to sit up when I found my wrists secured to the ground by ethereal wisps of yellowish light. Shunae sprung to her feet. I could hear the crowd give a collective gasp as she raised her hands over her head, ready to start hitting the area on my torso designated for earning points.

My body ached as her magic lanced out and struck me twice in quick succession, earning her two hits in less than five minutes.

"Two hits to zero," an announcer's voice boomed through the stadium.

This match would be over if I didn't figure out a way to fight back. Shunae danced away from me, clearly playing this up and looking to put on a show for the audience. I craned my neck, trying to scan the crowd for Gethin or Emerys' faces. I finally found Emerys amongst the crowd, her hood still obscuring her face. Our gazes met and I could feel her presence with me.

"You have to believe in yourself, like I do." I heard her voice in my head. *"Like your Aunt Nim did."*

For a split second, I could have sworn Aunt Nim stood beside Emerys, giving me an encouraging smile. If I couldn't at least make it through this round, and I didn't give it my all, Aunt Nim's death would mean nothing. I couldn't do that to the memory of the woman who'd raised me. I didn't care that she'd been some kind of traitor by defying orders and taking me through the portal rather kill me. She was my family in all the ways that mattered and I owed it to her to do this.

I turned my attention to the magical bonds keeping me immobile. I'd never really been able to *see* magic before, but I suppose desperate times called for desperate measures. I watched the wisps undulate around my wrist, tightening against my skin whenever I tried to flex my hand. It was beautiful in its simplicity. I'd never unraveled someone else's magic before either, but it was as if I could see the intricacies of the spell, just the tiniest loose thread in the weave of Shunae's intent. I tightened my left hand into a fist, envisioning myself giving that thread a firm pull.

Without realizing it, I'd poured my own will into the equation, the taste of lime tickling the back of my throat as the binds unraveled themselves. The gasp that went up from the crowd meant I wasn't the only one taking notice that I was now free to stand on my feet.

"You can do this," I said under my breath as I took stock of my surroundings.

Shunae still stood a short distance away, her mouth hanging open when our gazes met. I offered a shrug and began circling her. Gethin had noted she was right side dominant. I needed a way to get behind her without her seeing me though.

The fog from the qualifying trial came to mind. It had appeared more like a bit of Seelie magic, but surely I could do it, too. In my mind's eye, I pictured the pitch covered in a thick early morning fog. Power danced across my body, channeling until it coalesced into a thick cloud and Shunae vanished. More gasps from the crowd signaled they hadn't expected such a move from a witch either. For a moment panic threatened to immobilize me again, but I was the one in control this time.

Give me a little light.

I cupped my right hand down my thigh and a ball of greenish light coalesced. I directed it toward my feet, so it would cast just enough light for me to see by without betraying my location. The glow spread out, illuminating the ground ahead of me. Being able to navigate was one thing, but I couldn't earn any points if I couldn't find my opponent.

Lead me to her.

Lime permeated the fog around me and my heart skipped a beat as I worried it might be too much and give myself away. Nothing happened except the fog parted just enough off to my left that I got the hint.

Wanting this over as quickly as possible, part of me longed to charge her like she'd done me and just whale on her until the counts were over and I'd won. But that felt dirty and underhanded. Instead, I moved with stealth—or at least as much as I could traipsing through fog—until I'd determined I was within arm's reach of my opponent.

"Stop hiding!" Shunae shouted close to my ear. I heard more than saw her arms flailing around as she tried to fight her way through the fog.

I reached down to my little light and plucked a handful free before lobbing it at her back. It hit its target with a sizzle and Shunae let out a frustrated growl. The fog around us cleared enough for the crowd to see I'd landed my first hit.

"Two hits all," the announcer said in an unimpressed tone.

A loud crackle of lightning overhead drew my attention as the current arced through the air, disrupting the fog around us. It hissed and charred the ground around us.

"You really shouldn't bother fighting back. You're only going to lose," Shunae taunted as the lightning danced along her fingers.

"Everyone loves an underdog," I quipped and took a small step closer. "Besides, even if you beat me and make it back to the finals, Arthur did beat you pretty easily last year."

She let out a howl and lightning arced across her fingertips before it came crashing toward me. I didn't even realize my magic reacted until a blinding white barrier rose up around me, crashing against her attack like a wave. It turned her electric current back on her, slamming into her torso and sending her head over heels into the grass. The fog around us thinned enough for the referee and the assembled crowd to see the move.

"First point to Miss le Fey," the referee called, his voice booming through the stadium.

The crowd erupted into cheers. I stood stunned into immobility. My brain couldn't comprehend that these people, total strangers who didn't know me from a hole in the ground, were supporting me. Maybe they really did like an underdog after all.

I scanned the crowd, finally finding Gethin and Emerys. They both looked pleased and I caught Gethin mouthing, 'Three to go.' *Oh, shit.* The rules of this stupid tournament came flooding back to me. I'd merely survived the first attack. If I wanted to get through to the next round, I needed to keep fighting and score more points.

Before I managed to gather my wits about me, Shunae had regained her footing and charged at me, slamming her fist into my jaw. My vision blurred, dark spots popped across my field of vision, and my body listed to one side. The pain didn't immediately register as I caught my balance and raised my left hand to touch the spot where she'd slugged me. The act of acknowledging the injury was enough to make it throb at the barest hint of a touch.

The taste of copper filled my mouth as blood pooled within. I must have bitten my cheek or my tongue on impact. I managed to spit it out and wipe the red from my lips before she came toward me again. I wasn't the best in a fight, but I could hold my own for a few swings. But that wasn't what this was about. It was a battle of magic power, not who could hit hardest.

"Come on, you're better than this," I called to my opponent. "You want to beat me, do it the right way."

Before Shunae could react, the trumpet blared once echoing through the vast space. The referee approached me. "Get checked out," he ordered, giving me a rough shove toward where Gethin and Emerys stood watching.

"I am fine," I protested even as my jaw clicked unnaturally with every word.

The stern look from the referee made me think twice about arguing further. As I made my way to my support, I overheard the referee threaten to dock Shunae a penalty hit for her antics.

"You're doing brilliantly," Gethin praised as I sat down between them and accepted the ice pack he held out.

"Dumb luck," I answered and winced as I touched it to my jaw.

"Let me see," Emerys said, gently probing at the spot. After a moment and a soft, "Hmm ..." She continued, "It doesn't appear broken. Perhaps a little out of alignment. I can heal the injury, but it may hurt."

"Already hurts," I reminded her.

She waved her hand in front of my face and the pain grew sharp and stabbing to the point of taking my breath away. It subsided just as quickly and I felt the lump on my jaw recede.

"You need to conserve your strength and power. She will run you ragged if you let her," Emerys coached.

"Remember, get behind her," Gethin said as I stood. "Turning her magic back on her was a great move by the way."

I didn't have time to tell him it had been a fluke. As I stepped onto the pitch again, I couldn't help but fear I was about to get the shit beat out of me.

***

I GLANCED at the scoreboard through the sweat and blood dripping down my brow. Time had lost all meaning and we were now tied at three points each. Every breath brought me closer to the brink of exhaustion and total collapse. But I could hear Gethin's voice in the back of my head repeating, *Just one more point.'* That was all I needed and this would be over. Across the pitch, Shunae sported a few bruises and cuts herself. I hadn't meant to draw blood, but my magic had grown a bit erratic the more tired I became. The calm I'd found in the cave was deserting me now.

The referee blew his trumpet again and we stepped back into the center of the pitch. The crowd had begun to grow restless the longer it took to decide a victor. Somehow, I'd managed to get a large portion of the crowd on my side. But even their cheers were more muted now.

Shunae began pacing the grass across from me, planning her next move. I couldn't take this much longer. I swayed on my feet. I wiped more sweat and blood out of my eyes as my vision began to turn red.

The fog had worked well to conceal me before. Maybe I could do it one last time. I clenched my fists tight at my sides and poured out as much will as I could to conceal my location. The fog rolled in thinner this time, but it still blinded me. By the frustrated grunt ahead of me, it had for the moment obscured me from my opponent.

Bright bursts of light erupted between us as Shunae fought to burn the clouds away. As approaches went, it wasn't a bad idea. Besides, she had a hell of a lot more stamina than me and a decent chance of gaining enough of a view to send volleys of power in my direction. As I shuffled backwards, a thought occurred to me.

The qualifying trial.

The image of the land mine flashed before me. If everything Gethin had told me was true, then it was possible Shunae had never seen that particular trick before. The key would be to set the trigger, so it wouldn't actually injure her. I watched more flashes of light erupt through the fog as Shunae made her approach.

Crouching down low, I pressed my hands into the grass to my left. In my mind's eye, I pictured a device set to trigger ten seconds after weight was applied, whether that weight shifted or not.

Turn her magic back on her.

My magic swelled around me, pulling power from the fog I was struggling to sustain. A tiny device popped into existence beneath my fingers. The fog cleared. I scurried backwards on my hands and feet just as Shunae loomed high above me.

Our eyes met just as the *'click'* of the mine triggered under her weight. Her fiery gaze turned earthward even as her hands burned bright with more fluorescent magic. I was as prone as I could get, frozen in place out of fear and a morbid sense of curiosity. I wanted to see if what I'd done actually worked. In my head I counted down.

Ten ...

Nine ...

Eight ...

Seven ...

Six ...

Five ...

Four...

Three ...

Two ...

Shunae let loose all of the power she'd coalesced into her hands, sending it straight at my head. I braced for the impact, only to hear a louder boom as the mine launched her into the air. I watched, mouth agape as the magic she'd intended for me stopped mere inches from my face before rebounding on her. The pressure of her magic colliding with her body knocked her straight to the ground with a meaty 'thump.'

The referee appeared through the dissipating fog and knelt beside Shunae. For one horrible moment I feared my magic had gone wrong again and I'd somehow killed her.

She sat up with her uniform glowing from the three clear hits. She glared daggers at me. I couldn't stop the whoop of relief that ripped from my throat that she was still alive.

"Match point goes to Miss le Fey," the referee announced.

Before I knew it, Gethin had raced onto the pitch and hauled me to my feet. Emerys joined us using a more respectable pace, still keeping her head down. The scoreboard changed to reflect I'd earned the final point.

After regaining her composure, Shunae approached and offered her hand. "Good match," she said.

I hesitated to return the gesture for a moment before shaking. "Yeah you, too. Sorry about the trash talk earlier."

She gave me a small smile. "All part of the game. Hope that beginner's luck holds for you. Because you're going to need it."

All around us, the crowd chanted my name. For the briefest of moments, I actually believed I could win this whole damn thing.

TWELVE

That buzz of invincibility from the end of the match lasted until I'd made it back to my room and collapsed on the bed. I sank into the pillows and the softness of the mattress and closed my eyes.

"I've got some ideas ..." Gethin began as he entered the room.

"Sleep first," I mumbled into the pillow.

"It's not even two in the afternoon," he pointed out.

I rolled over so that I could look up at him. "And I just did more magic in the last few hours than I've done in my entire fucking life ..."

"Oh, yeah ... I guess that's true." He pivoted and

tugged the curtains closed. "A few hours' sleep is probably a good idea then."

I gave a tired nod and rolled back over, letting the comfort of the bed beneath lull me to sleep. When I opened my eyes again, the room was dark. I could hear the sound of someone scribbling against paper nearby and I craned my neck to find Gethin jotting down notes.

"What time is it?" I asked, my mouth feeling full of cotton.

He spun in the chair. "A little after seven. They're having a mixer event with drinks until midnight tonight. You ought to make an appearance."

I wanted to beg off, but the way he looked at me suggested this was not an optional thing. "Please tell me I can just wear whatever I want."

"Don't worry, you don't have to go around in a ridiculous fancy dress or anything," he said and I heaved an audible sigh of relief.

I levered myself out of the bed and darted for the shower. Stepping out fifteen minutes later, I felt refreshed. Somehow, the scrapes and bruises I'd incurred during the match didn't look nearly as noticeable. I tugged on a pair of jeans and an off the shoulder top in a deep forest green that matched the pair of Doc Martins I wore.

"You're coming, aren't you?" I paused at the doorway when Gethin didn't stand up.

"It's just for the participants. But I'll be around if you need me." He didn't look happy with the fact he wasn't coming. I chalked it up to tournament envy.

"But I don't know anyone. Besides, I don't want to say the wrong thing or insult the wrong person and ruin everything."

"Just keep conversations to small talk then," he said, offering what I'm sure he thought was a reassuring smile. He scooped up the pin I'd removed from my uniform and he tossed it overhand to me before gesturing for me to secure it on my collar. "Tomorrow, we'll start pepping for your quarter finals match." He made a shooing motion, signaling the discussion was over.

I fastened the pin to my shirt and sucked in a deep breath as I left the room behind. Finding the gathering wasn't difficult. A large tent sat erected in the center of the lodging area. Music filtered through the air and six-foot-tall torches lit the path to the entrance. I strolled up, expecting to be questioned about my right to be there, but no one guarded the entryway.

The moment I stepped into the tent; the cacophony of sound overloaded my hearing. The lights dancing of their own accord at the top of the tent were more vibrant than the sun. I blinked, trying to clear my vision. At least there didn't appear to be any of whatever passed for paparazzi in Camelot lurking around in the hopes of snapping an unflattering picture of the competitors.

"You look a bit lost," an alto voice called from my right. Thankfully, my ears had finally adjusted to the noise level inside the tent.

I turned to find a woman about my age with a deep complexion standing beside me. She sported a pin on her lapel that I'd filed away in my mind as the dragon delegation.

"Is it that obvious?" I let out a hiccup of nervous laughter.

"I hate these things, too," she said and downed the dregs from her glass. "I'm Talia by the way."

"Morgan."

"I haven't seen you in a tournament before," Talia noted as we moved away from the entrance to a less occupied area of the tent.

"Uh, yeah. This is my first time," I said, trying to heed Gethin's suggestion of small talk. "First time I qualified."

"The qualifying trial can be brutal," she agreed. "I almost didn't make it this year."

"It's a lot harder than I expected. The matches I mean," I said, feeling awkward as I watched the other participants clustered together in little groups of threes and fours. I spotted one of the taller fae guys towering over everyone else. Our gazes met and a shiver danced down my spine. He gave me a toothy grin, but it only served to accentuate the sharpness of his jawline and the haughty expression in his eyes.

"Who is that?" I asked, nudging Talia to direct her attention.

"That is Gunter Forsythe. One of the Seelie's most accomplished spell casters. It was actually supposed to be him against Arthur last year, but he went out with a shoulder injury and Shunae won their match by default."

"Hope I don't ever have to be anywhere near him."

Talia let out a snort. "You're joking right?"

I shook my head. "Clearly, I'm missing something."

"You haven't checked the bracket since your match, have you? He's who you'll be facing in your quarter finals match."

"Oh, fuck me."

"It was his left shoulder. She had very nearly

severed every ligament and tendon keeping his arm attached," she offered with a shrug. "I heard he's been rehabbing it all year."

"He looks like he could bench press me one handed with his eyes closed," I groaned. Maybe that's why Gethin had been so determined to go over strategies already.

"I'd say it's just a bit of fun, but this year is a lot more stressful with the coronation coming up," Talia said.

"Arthur's coronation?" I guessed.

"That's the one."

"Can I ask you something, what may sound like a stupid question?"

She turned, so her back was to Gunter and the gaggle surrounding him. "Why not?"

"Pretend for a second I know absolutely nothing about the political climate in Camelot. Why is Arthur taking the throne when the queen looks perfectly capable of ruling?"

She fixed me with a perplexed look before finally shrugging it off and answering. "Most monarchs around here don't rule until they're ancient. Not anymore anyway. It's a way to keep things fresh. New ideas and all that."

It made a certain sort of sense, but I still couldn't

fathom the practicality of it. Then again, I'd been raised in a place where we'd had the same ruling monarch my entire life.

"And he wants that responsibility?"

As if our conversation had drawn him close, Arthur appeared among the throng of other participants and servers. Everyone around the prince gave him a respectable berth. He carried a glass of something red in one hand as he walked by us toward the entrance of the tent.

"He'd have taken the crown at eighteen if they had let him. That man has been angling for power his whole life." Talia looked down at her empty glass. "I need a refill. Want a drink?"

"I'd love one."

For the next hour, I forced myself not to disparage the bartender. But the more alcohol I consumed, the harder it became not to criticize everything he did.

"You've really got a thing for alcohol," Talia noted.

"I'm a bartender by trade. Not exactly what I'd planned for my life, but I know how to make drinks and this stuff … it would never pass as a drink where I'm from."

"Remind me to have you make me a drink sometime."

Heat crept up my neck at the way she looked at me. *Is she flirting with me?* It wouldn't be the first time a drunk woman had made a pass at me, but this felt different. I did my best to laugh it off, but excused myself as quickly as I could. I'd mingled enough for one night.

***

THAT NIGHT, images of Gunter swirled in my alcohol-addled brain and I woke a little before sunrise in a cold sweat. Gethin snored softly in the other bed. I knew he'd be awake soon enough and ready to rehash yesterday's match, but I wasn't ready for strategy talk.

I really wanted to talk to Emerys, but had no idea how to get in touch with her. And it wasn't like I could just hop on the train back to her cabin at a moment's notice. I had to follow the rules of the tournament. I paced the short distance from the edge of the bed to the front window and back several times before I stopped. My ears perked up at the sound of approaching footsteps. They stopped outside our door and my heart skipped a beat.

Who would be paying me a visit this early?

I yanked the door open before the visitor had a chance to knock. I found Emerys standing on the other side of the threshold. "I was just trying to think of a way to get in touch with you," I said in a hushed tone, so as not to wake Gethin.

"Why don't we take a walk? I suspect you have some things on your mind you wish to discuss."

"Are you sure mindreading isn't one of your magical talents?" It was only partly a joke.

She just gave me a tight-lipped smile and we headed out of the lodging area and toward the courtyard. Workers were busy cleaning up from the prior days' festivities. I could already hear the distant chatter of attendees queuing to get to their seats and maybe catch a glimpse of their favorite participant.

"You did well yesterday," Emerys complimented.

"I felt like I had no idea what I was doing. And tomorrow I'm supposed to face some Seelie bloke who looks like he could break me in half without even trying."

"I believe you will rise to the occasion. The world, as I am sure you know, must exist in a balance between light and dark. I truly believe Arthur's existence in Camelot these last three decades tipped the scales against us. You being here and succeeding in this tournament is the first step in setting the scales to rights."

"I know you keep saying that it's my destiny. But not everything can be preordained like that. Not with me anyway."

"You were able to access your magic freely during your match. That is not something you were able to do before. Your control is growing. If you were anyone else, that would have taken years of training and discipline. But you are meant to be here, to take back your place in this kingdom, and the world around you knows it."

In that moment I realized she had never considered an outcome where I failed. I wanted to point out that she should be ready for the inevitable. My luck such as it was, was bound to run out eventually. But I couldn't deny that she had a point. My magic had been far easier to access in the heat of the match than ever before. And I'd managed to win on my own merit and not with dirty tricks either.

I didn't recognize where we were until the sudden pressure in my chest caught my breath. My body lurched to one side and I found myself standing a meter from the stone in which Excalibur sat encased. My vision tunneled until all I saw was the sword. The hilt glittered an alluring blue in the early morning sunlight. It called to me even without words and my feet moved of their own accord until a firm hand on my shoulder halted my forward progress.

"We cannot be seen here," Emerys urged. "There are too many prying eyes."

"I—I ... didn't mean to. I just got this sort of feeling and then I was just here. I swear, I think the sword's calling to me."

"And you doubt your lineage and your right to be here? That sword can sense Pendragon blood and it must be screaming out for you. Soon enough you can reclaim what's yours, but not yet."

As we turned to head back to the competitors' lodging area, I thought I spotted a cluster of activity at the far end of the courtyard. The doors opened and the queen stepped out in casual clothes, carrying an oversized mug of coffee. In that moment she looked like any woman in her sixties just enjoying the sunrise. I could see myself in the way she leaned one hip against a nearby support column as she watched the people around her work.

Beside me, I heard Emerys' breath hitch in her throat. I glanced over to see her also staring at the queen, a wistful expression on her face. "Even from here, I can see so much of you in her."

"It's strange, but I can, too," I murmured. After a moment, I added, "She can't really hold a grudge this long." Emerys turned away and I followed after her, leaving the courtyard behind. "She's probably forgotten all about it."

"I'm afraid until the truth comes out, I won't be welcome back here." The longing in her expression was palpable. "I must admit, I am ready to come home. You may feel my belief in your skills and what you will accomplish is misguided, but it isn't just your homecoming I have dreamt of all these years ..."

No pressure.

"I'll do everything I can to bring us both home then."

That started with finding Gethin, so we could plan how I was going to make it past the quarter finals and one step closer to facing off against Arthur.

THIRTEEN

W e'd left the lodging complex behind. Thanks to Gethin's secret passage knowledge, we'd managed to sneak off the grounds without being seen. We caught the train back to Emerys' cabin. She'd promised we would return to Camelot in time for my match the next morning. At least I wouldn't have to sit around waiting and obsessing over how my next match would play out.

Even after just a few days in the city, surrounded by all of the people and festivities, being back near the lake had a more calming effect than I'd anticipated. I'd never been a country girl. Aunt Nim and I had always lived in London. Yet the stillness near Emerys' cabin amplified my connection to the magic around me in a way I couldn't quite feel in more urban areas.

"So, you've probably heard that Gunter is a bit of a brute," Gethin said as we stood inside the training room behind Emerys' cabin.

"Yeah. But I also heard he nearly lost an arm last year and that could be a weak point."

"It was pretty gruesome actually." He blanched. "Anyway, going after his weak side isn't a bad move. But you're going to need to be prepared. Seelies are naturally connected to nature and they use it to their advantage."

"I thought everyone was. That's where magic comes from, right? It's in everything and we tap into it."

"That is true, but they've got sort of an affinity for it. Like they could grow roots around your legs in three seconds flat before you've even had a chance to devise a way to protect yourself."

"Brilliant. Well, I mean, I can make things grow, too. Well ... sometimes anyway."

"That fog trick you pulled against Shunae was pretty effective. I'd definitely give that one a go."

"I don't want to be a one trick pony," I muttered.

"Look ... normally, I'd say you're right. But right now, your magic is still unpredictable. The more you use it here, the more control you gain, and the more versatile it becomes. Until then, go with what seems to work."

"Creating the fog might be simple. But I still haven't figured out a good way to see where I'm going and find my opponent without giving my own location away."

"That is a problem we can solve." The pallor of his cheeks brightened and his eyes shone with excitement. "Why don't you show me what you've been doing so far?"

I closed my eyes, allowing my mind to fill with an image of the fog, rolling in across the landscape, enveloping us completely. I could feel the weight of the damp air pressing in against my body. When I opened my eyes, our surroundings were completely obscured.

"Gethin?" I called.

"I'm here." I heard his voice from somewhere off to my left. I resisted the urge to reach out my hand in a blind grab.

"What do I do now?" I asked.

"Whatever you did before to light your way."

I lifted my right hand until I could almost distinguish the outline of my fingers through the fog and let a bit of power slip out. A gauzy green globe of light erupted from my hand, rising to burn away the fog directly in front of me.

"I think I see where you are," Gethin said and a moment later, the light reflected off the rims of his glasses, giving him an almost eerie glow.

"That's the problem," I groaned.

"Obviously, you need the light to be able to see where you're going. But do you need it to be so overt?"

"I don't follow."

"You've got this big old blob of light just hanging around you like a torch. What if, instead of casting the light outwardly to allow you to see, you focused it from your eyes?"

"Like give myself magically enhanced vision?"

"Why not?"

"Oh ... maybe because with my luck, I'd manage to screw it up and blind myself. Or I'd do the opposite and my vision would be so intensified that I'd be able to see too much."

"Don't let the fear of what might be get in your way. You are in control of the magic. Not the other way around, Morgan. You can do this."

He took a few steps back beyond the perimeter of the glow of my light source and vanished completely. I was terrified to try what he'd asked and yet, it made a lot of sense. It would allow me to see without giving away my position. Practically speaking, that was a useful trick to have up my sleeve even if I wasn't about to go fight a giant brute for my claim to fame.

"Focus," I said and inhaled a deep breath.

The light around me faded and I closed my eyes again. Out of instinct, my hands clenched into tight fists. But tightening up wasn't the answer. I forced my fingers to uncurl and for my hands to hang loosely at my sides. I needed to welcome the magic and let it be a part of me.

Let me see through the fog.

The scent of limes coated the inside of my nose and the backs of my eyes burned and itched for a moment before the irritation subsided. Time to see if this really worked. When I opened my eyes this time, the fog took on a greenish tinge and I could see the outline of Gethin's body a few paces away.

"Have you done it yet?" Gethin called.

I didn't answer. Instead, I crept around, flanking his left side before jumping and tackling him to the ground with a loud 'oomph.' I let out a squeal of excitement that I'd managed it and the fog faded, taking my enhanced vision along with it.

"I'd say that's one problem solved," Gethin said as he struggled to sit up.

As soon as our surroundings returned to normal, my head began pounding and my vision blurred. I managed to push myself up against one of the walls and sit with my head in my hands, taking deep, steadying breaths.

"Don't think my body liked me doing that," I said when the dizziness and the aching subsided a few minutes later.

"Magic always comes with a price," Gethin said softly.

"You'd think, if I'm really meant to make it to the finals and be this hero that you all think I am, the universe might cut me a fucking break. What good am I to anyone if I pass out from a bloody migraine in the middle of a match?"

"We just need to keep practicing. The more you do it, the less strain it's going to put on your body."

"Ugh! That makes no sense," I snapped.

"You practice a move over and over until you've mastered it. Along the way, you're bound to have strained muscles, because your body's not used to you using it in that way. Same goes for magic. Let's get some food in you and then we'll go again."

I HATED TO ADMIT IT, but Gethin was right. The more I practiced, the less agony I wound up in at the end. By the time the sun was making its descent over the trees into evening, I could sustain both the fog and my enhanced sight for up to five minutes without it knocking me flat on my arse afterward.

"He's going to try and rip me apart, isn't he?" I asked as we sat at the table, drinking coffee.

"He's big, but he's kind of slow too. He likes to use the fact he's so tall to intimidate other people. Use that your advantage."

"Right, well we should be getting back. A good night's sleep couldn't hurt before a big match," I said, downing the dregs of my drink.

"Yeah, let me just clean up here," Gethin said and swiped the empty mug from my hand.

I moved to stand in the doorway, staring out at the grass and trees beyond the cabin. I was once again struck by the sense that there was something missing. I felt the weight of my useless phone in my pocket. The frustration that I had so much to share with Julayne and couldn't reach her brought tears to my eyes.

"We can go," Gethin said from behind me. I

didn't move. He shifted to stand beside me and I felt his hand on my bicep. "What is it?"

"I just can't believe all of this is actually happening and my best friend isn't here to share it with me. She would love all of this."

"I know you feel like everyone important to you is missing out on this," he said. "I wish I knew a way to connect the two of you across realms, but that is clearly not my skillset."

"You could be a real mate and find someone who can," I said, nudging him in the ribs.

"I don't know, Morgan. That feels a little dangerous."

"How is making a phone call to my world dangerous?"

"Because not everyone knows that there are other realms out there. And the sort of people that do, aren't exactly who you want to entrust the personal information of the rightful heir of Camelot."

"You're being paranoid. Look, I'm not expecting you to work miracles. Just see what you can find. I mean, Emerys is hundreds of years old. She's bound to know if there's anyone who has the knowledge."

"She's not going to be happy, but I'll try." He

muttered half-heartedly. "Come on, like you said before, we'd better get back."

As we left the cabin behind, I felt the tiny hairs on the backs of my arms bristle. I glanced over my shoulder, but nothing obvious stuck out to me. Still, I couldn't shake the sensation of being watched.

Let me see.

My vision sharpened like I'd been practicing all afternoon. I cast my gaze skyward, but nothing appeared out of the ordinary. When I turned my attention back to the ground, I could see the vague outline of something moving in the trees, traveling away from us. Whatever it was looked to be cloaked. Even when I squinted, I couldn't make out more than a general humanoid shape.

"What is it?" Gethin's question brought my focus back to the moment and my enhanced sight receded.

"Maybe nothing, but I think something or someone was spying on us."

He spun to face the way we'd come, his shoulder muscles tensing with anxiety. Maybe it was the very last vestiges of my vision spell, but I could swear I saw magic ripple off his skin, washing over both of us.

"What'd you just do?" I asked as my equilibrium faltered.

"Made it so we're difficult to follow now. Just stick close to me." He looped his arm through mine for good measure as we headed on our way.

He kept the spell going even after we'd made it to the train and were aboard, hurtling back toward the city. The car was mostly empty. Apparently most people were either already in Camelot for the duration of the tournament or weren't going anywhere near the place. That didn't mean there wouldn't be prying eyes to report that we'd snuck off.

"So, this friend of yours, what's she like?" Gethin broached.

"Jules? She's brilliant. One of the best witches I've ever met. It's like everything comes easy to her, with magic."

"Besides her magic, tell me one thing about her that makes you like her?"

"She's loyal. She's always had my back. We met in grammar school and lived in the same complex for a while, too. Magic wasn't a secret where we grew up. But that didn't mean you wouldn't get picked on for not being able to do it, or do it well. I'm not ashamed to admit, she got me out of a few scrapes back then with some bullies."

"They didn't believe you were destined to rule a far off kingdom?"

"No. But she never stopped believing in that truth. That's why it's killing me she's not here to see everything and experience it all with me. It feels as if I've gone and just left her behind."

"Well, I mean, you were literally under attack. From what you said, there wasn't much time to do anything else."

"Maybe I should have insisted she come with us?"

"I will see what I can do about your phone situation. You need to focus on beating Gunter in the morning."

As the train pulled into the station, I couldn't dispel the sense of foreboding settling over me. I wanted to believe everything would go my way in the morning. That I'd be able to beat Gunter and make it to the semi-finals. It would make a brilliant tale to share with Julayne when I saw her again. But nothing was guaranteed, I knew that better than anyone.

We managed to make it back to the grounds unnoticed and Gethin finally dropped his spell. He unhooked his arm from mine and we walked at a slow pace, hoping it would appear we had been around the whole time.

"Excuse me," a high-pitched voice called as we reached the competitors' lodging.

I turned to find a young girl with a pair of thick-lensed glasses standing there, a small book and pen in hand. I looked around, expecting someone more important than me holding her attention, but we were the only people in the child's immediate line of sight.

"Uh ... hi there," I greeted.

"You're in the tournament," she squeaked.

"That's right. I'm Morgan."

She held up her book and pen. "Can I have your autograph?"

I gaped at her in disbelief. I'd only made it through one round. Sure, I'd beaten the prior year's runner up, but that wasn't a huge upset. Why would she want my autograph? "Are you sure?"

She nodded. "I'm collecting autographs of all the participants to commemorate coming to my first tournament."

I cast a sideways look at Gethin. He shrugged, not knowing how else to proceed either. "Yeah, alright."

I took the book and flipped to a blank page. I took a moment to see if she'd landed Arthur's yet.

He was still missing from her count it would appear. "Who should I make this out to?"

"Tillie with an ie at the end."

"To Tillie, with an ie at the end. Thanks for being a fan," I said as I signed her book and handed it back.

She examined my signature up close, tracing her finger along the scrawled ink. She locked up and beamed at me. "Thanks!"

I gave her a little wave as she ran off to join a woman in a blue dress. Tillie offered a wave back before they went on their way.

"I think the universe is trying to give you a signal to keep your chin up. People are going to have your back here, too," Gethin whispered in my ear.

I let Tillie's admiration buoy me the rest of the day. I just had to keep that positivity as I faced off against Gunter in the morning. So much easier said than done.

FOURTEEN

The tension in the air as I marched out to the pitch the next morning was palpable. People were paying attention to me now. I'd already shown I could hold my own against one of the strongest witches in the tournament. Even if no one said anything, I could feel the heavy weight of expectation settle over my shoulders.

"Remember, you're meant for this," Gethin whispered in my ear before I walked out to face Gunter.

Even though I'd seen him kind of up close a few nights ago, I was still struck by just how tall he was compared to me. I barely came up to his navel. His biceps bulged twice the size of just one of my arms. He opened his mouth in a wicked grin, and I could swear his teeth were pointed. There was a glint of malice in his eyes when our gazes met across the arena.

The referee, a thin woman, with a beaklike nose and hair resembling the texture of candy floss with the color of a spider's web, marched out between us. She looked up at Gunter and then turned her focus to me. "I want a clean match."

She backed out of the way and blew the trumpet twice before calling, "Begin." I took a few slow steps to the right, forcing him to mirror me. I had no doubt he had stamina for days. Outlasting him wasn't going to be the answer in this fight. I needed to go for quick, easy hits to score my four points.

"You look weak, little witch," Gunter called in a deep bass voice and smirked. "I'm going to enjoy crushing you."

"I've dealt with plenty of blokes like you. Haven't you heard that the bigger and dumber they are, the harder they fall?" I quipped back.

He tightened his hands into fists, like he was going to slam one into my face. I could hear his knuckles pop and crack as he did so. Somehow, I held my focus even when my stomach did a flop as my mind imagined him landing a blow. To my surprise, he didn't strike.

Time to get this over with.

I flexed my fingers, spreading them wide at my sides and felt my magic cascade over my body like a raging river. For a split second, panic set in. The fear that my magic would come out untamed and uncontrolled paralyzed me. It made everything around me slow down to half speed.

But my power didn't overwhelm me, or come pouring out. It just wrapped around me, ready and eager to enact my will. I pictured the same fog rolling in and the spell for my eyes I'd practiced with Gethin yesterday in my head. When I opened my eyes, everything around us had vanished, enveloped in a thick cloud. I blinked twice to get used to my magically enhanced vision. I could barely make out Gunter's looming form a few feet away. The outline of his body turned around and I heard angry grunts of frustration as he swung his meaty fists through the air at an alarming approximation of my head height.

I took advantage of his disorientation and turned my attention to the ground beneath my feet. Several approaches ran through my mind. I could try and summon up something like lightning or fire to lob his way and score a few hits. But that wasn't exactly something I was experienced doing. I could try and confine him with the surrounding fog and earth beneath our feet. But it was entirely possible his connection to nature would overwhelm mine and backfire.

What I really needed was a back-up. Something that could take a few hits for me and keep him distracted while I came up with a more workable plan. The image of the plant golem from my qualifying round came to mind. It wasn't a half-bad idea, except for being made of plants.

"Use your magic," I heard Emerys' voice in my head.

Glancing in the direction she and Gethin had settled, I could swear I saw her give a small nod. I wasn't sure she was supposed to be giving me hints, but I'd take all the help I could get.

I have no idea if this is going to work.

I turned my focus inward, to the core of my magic. I felt it pulsing within me, pouring out through every inch of my body to fuel the fog. In my mind's eye, I watched myself reach into the pulsating beam of magic and tugged some strands away from the whole. My mental self began weaving the magic together and between one breath and the next it took on human form.

Mentally I flicked its fingers and the magically

woven figure stepped forward, approaching my viewpoint. It was definitely female—I could make out the slope of breasts and the curve of hips, but she had no other defining features. She was pure energy—magic and that's all she needed to be.

"Let's see if this works," I said.

When I opened my eyes again, the faceless energy golem stood beside me. Through the fog I could make out Gunter, moving in a methodical search pattern with his fists still held high. I could also make out unnatural spikes protruding from his fingers. *Wonderful.*

Realizing talking to my golem aloud would defeat the purpose of trying to conceal my location, I turned and thought my question really hard. *'Can you hear me?'* The golem nodded her head. God, magic gobsmacked me sometimes. I gestured for her to flank Gunter as I went around the other direction. Once we were on either side of him, I urged the fog to lift.

The sudden change in his visual field was enough to disrupt Gunter's forward progress. It also gave me a chance to take stock of the fact he'd grown rose thorns through his skin. They glistened, promising all manner of pain if I wasn't careful.

'Get him.'

I wasn't expecting the golem to literally jump on Gunter's back, but that's exactly what she did. She wrapped her limbs around his torso, elongating them as she did so, making contact with all the parts of his uniform that registered hits.

"Dirty witch," Gunter howled as he tried to shake the golem free.

I barely registered the referee calling out that I'd managed to win the first point. Not just one hit, but the entire point. Getting hits in would be so much easier if Gunter was stationary. Relying on nature was a risk, but it was one I was willing to take. I focused on the ground at his feet, urging it to swell, to envelope his feet as if stuck in mud, and harden again.

It fought my intent, sending pangs through the base of my skull. Maybe trying to sustain multiple spells at once wasn't such a good idea. The golem's presence flickered momentarily as I strained to get nature to cooperate.

All at once, something stung my left cheek. The spell I'd been trying to work crumbled as I lifted a hand to feel one of Gunter's thorns poking out of my face. That side of my face went numb as I plucked the thorn free. My vision went fuzzy and my head swam. Did this knobhead just *poison* me? The golem vanished from his back. I felt a rush of power as the magic reabsorbed into my body, redirecting its objective without me having to ask. Unfortunately for me, while I took the time to try and stave off the disorientation, Gunter sent a series of eerily purple globs of energy hurtling at my torso. They landed, knocking the air from my lungs and I staggered backward.

"One point all," the referee announced.

Gunter didn't even let me catch my breath before he bore down on me. That same purple energy crackled along his forearms and glinted in his eyes. "We aren't going to fail again," he hissed as he reached one meaty hand for my throat.

I managed to scramble beyond his grasp, doing an awkward half-roll to get out of range. As I did so, I spotted one of Gunter's entourage watching me intently. The slant of his jaw and the look in his eyes registered after a moment and I froze. He looked like one of the soldiers who'd killed Aunt Nim. But that wasn't possible. We'd evaded them on the ferry and they didn't follow us. Even still, the look the Seelie gave me was pure hatred.

"Behind you!" someone yelled.

I spun to find Gunter at my back again. I wasn't fast enough to avoid him this time. His hand tightened around my throat, hoisting me off the ground. Air fled my lungs and black spots danced in my vision. It appeared to go grey at the edges faster this time.

Time slowed and I could feel my heartbeat begin to slow the more he squeezed. Maybe it would be better to just let him choke me out. The pressure of being someone I still didn't quite believe I was meant to be wouldn't exist anymore. That would be nice.

'Fight back!'

Aunt Nim's voice rang sharply in my head. It was almost certainly a hallucination from my oxygen-deprived brain. And yet, just hearing her voice was enough to snap me out of giving up. I tried to move my arms, to raise my fingers, and claw at his hands that continued to squeeze my throat, but it was as if I moved in slow motion. I couldn't even be sure my body was actually responding to the weak signals my brain was sending out.

Something shrill sounded off in the distance. I couldn't make myself focus on it. Not when I had more important things to do like survive being choked to death. There was some commotion around us, but my vision continued to turn grey and hazy.

Without warning, the pressure on my throat ceased and my legs crumpled beneath me as I fell to the ground. I coughed, choking as air passed through my strained airway. I felt two pairs of hands on my back.

"Come on, let's get you up," Gethin said in my ear.

All I could do was nod mutely as I coughed and sucked in much needed oxygen. By the time we'd reached the side of the pitch, my vision was mostly restored, as was my hearing. I could make out that the crowd was angry about something.

"He ... tried ... to kill ..." I rasped.

"We know. Everyone saw. The referee is giving him a dressing down right now. Sounds like they might give you a penalty point," Gethin explained as he pressed a damp cloth to my throat. The moisture literally melted into my skin, reaching my aching throat faster than drinking water. And it hurt a hell of a lot less.

"Penalty point?" I croaked.

"Essentially, because he wasn't using magic on you, he forfeited his chance at his next point. You'd be up two to one," Gethin answered.

That would mean I only needed to survive getting two more points to win and for this whole match to be over. Despite that it still felt like it would be ages before it was finished. Emerys came into view, plucking my wrist and checking my pulse.

"That was a clever trick with the golem," she noted with a hint of pride.

"Thanks. Wasn't sure it would work." The base of my skull ached with another oncoming magic burnout headache. "Think I tried too many things though and it sort of backfired."

"You tried to manipulate the earth around him. He is Seelie," Emerys said.

"I know. It was a risk, but I had to try."

"Binding him up isn't a bad move. Just maybe use something that's not made of nature?" Gethin suggested.

"Penalty point against Mr. Forsythe," the referee announced. "The score is now two points to one, Miss le Fey."

"If all else fails, lure him onto a landmine," Gethin said cheerily and helped me to my feet.

I wasn't going to risk earning a penalty point against me and prolonging matters. I gave my friend a tight-lipped nod as I returned to the pitch and tried to put together some semblance of a plan of attack this time around. Gunter stopped a few paces from me and I caught something glint off his wrist.

A silver band shone in the sunlight when he lifted his hand. Oh wait, that just might work.

"You can do this," I whispered under my breath.

I wasn't going to leave myself open to a direct attack from him again if I could help it. I held up one hand and summoned a barrier of opaque bluish-green energy. He lobbed a fireball my way and the shield deflected it. It narrowly avoided hitting him in the shin. Time to see if I could be a metal worker.

With my other hand, I made a grasping motion in his direction. In my head, I pictured the band around his hand thinning out, elongating, and turning into a fine chained mesh that was strong as steel. I envisioned it wrapping around his body and keeping him still.

Gunter sent another fireball hurtling toward me. It bounced against my shield and this time landed at his feet, sizzling and smoking in the grass. The shield wavered for a moment before it solidified again. Fueling two spells simultaneously was defi-nitely a skill I needed to work on.

Two more white-hot spheres came barreling toward me. They collided with the shield and while it repelled one—sending it right into Gunter's left arm in the middle of the patch that registered hits—the second slipped through and I could smell singed hair as it grazed the side of my head before landing on the ground behind me.

Maybe trying to keep my magic in check was what was hurting me right now. I tried to let it loose. Remembering what it felt like that first day I'd tried to train with Gethin. Power poured out of me now and when I opened my eyes, the band on Gunter's wrist was gone, replaced by the mesh I'd been trying to conjure. I only needed five more hits to finish this.

'Make his magic rebound.'

I poured that intent into the chains around him as I sent sparks of power through the mesh. Everywhere they touched he jerked. I could see the frustration on his face as he tried to free himself, only to find the chains drawing tighter. I dropped the shield and poured that focus and energy into getting those last few hits in.

"Match to Miss le Fey," the referee's voice echoed across the pitch. The crowd cheered.

I fell to my knees and the chains binding Gunter vanished, melting back into the band around his wrist. Sweat beaded on every part of my body and my muscles shook from the match's effort. But I'd managed to make it through one more round.

I forced myself onto my feet and offered a hand

to the man who'd just tried to kill me. I plastered a fake smile on my lips for the photo op and he did the same. I scanned the stands behind Gunter, searching for the Seelie soldier I'd seen before, but he was gone. This match might be over, but something told me I was going to need to watch my back.

Part of me knew I should be preparing for the semi-final match, but I couldn't drag myself out of bed until almost night the next day. Mercifully, Gethin and Emerys had let me sleep. When I finally emerged from the depths of slumber, I felt only slightly rested. My body ached in places I didn't know could hurt.

"You need to keep up your strength," Gethin said, handing me a plate of food.

"I should just go back to bed," I grumbled, annoyed he'd dragged me down to the common area. Still, I accepted the food, poking at it with a fork absently.

"Normally, I'd agree. But the results from the

other quarter-final match are in. You're facing off against Princess Talia. You get to fight a dragon!"

Talia from the mixer was a princess? She'd been so friendly and ... *normal*. I didn't want to have to fight her. The sound of pure excitement in his voice made me perk up. "That's the part of the qualifying trial I failed at ... miserably. I just ran."

"Well, look at it this way, you've got a chance for a do-over."

"Dragons are massive. They can fly. And they've got impenetrable scales," I pointed out. Granted I was only certain of two of those points.

"You'd be surprised where they've got vulnerabilities. But most of the time during the tournament, dragon participants don't shift form. Besides, Talia is pretty chill, normally," Gethin noted, gesturing to a table on the far side of the room.

I spotted Talia across the commons space. In this light, I realized how much she reminded me of Taron. She lounged in a chair, one arm thrown over the back. She turned and caught me staring. Recognition registered on her face and she flashed me a smile and offered up a quick wave.

"Of all the people you've faced, she's probably your easiest competition," Gethin said, drawing my attention back to him.

"Seriously ... How do you suggest I beat her, then?"

"Honestly, just keep doing what you've been doing. Different combinations of things work. I mean that spell you did binding Gunter was awe inspired."

I shrugged, shoving food into my mouth. I barely registered the taste. "You told me to get creative and that's what I did."

"People are starting to notice. I mean the crowds have been talking about you all day. Most participants who make it this far on a regular basis have a set way of doing things. You're winging it and people like it."

"Hooray, I'm liked. My life is now complete," I deadpanned.

"Morgan, come on. This should be an ego boost for you. The people like you. That's part of what you need to happen if we're going to succeed with ... you know what." He was smart not to admit aloud in a crowded room that we were trying to unseat the crown prince.

"I know and it is nice to hear. But, mate, I'm exhausted. And if you haven't noticed, I don't do well without sleep."

"I had noticed that," he agreed before moving

his chair to sit beside me. He leaned in and lowered his voice. "I did manage to do a bit of asking around about your, uh ... other thing."

I stared at him in momentary confusion. He mimed holding a phone to his ear and it registered. "Did you find someone who could make my phone work here?"

"Yes, but it's going to be expensive. The kind of money I don't just have laying around."

"If you think I've got money, you're mistaken. I tend bar for a living and I lived with my aunt. Besides, I'm not even sure the money I do have would work here."

"I know you miss your friend, but maybe it's just better if we hold off on contacting her until after the tournament. Once you've claimed the throne, you'll have plenty of funds and besides, I'm sure the court has people who could figure it out for you."

Before I could respond, the doors behind us opened and Arthur walked in. A few of the other participants sporting Camelot's crest stood upon his arrival. Though I didn't move a muscle. He scanned the room, his gaze finally landing on me. He sauntered over and pulled up a chair, sitting at our table without invitation.

"You're making quite the impression with the populace," he said, chin propped in one hand.

"Just lucky I suppose," I answered, keeping a firm grip on the fork in my hand.

"I have to admit, I had good money on Gunter beating you in a landslide."

The fact he'd bet against me and lost gave me a small sense of satisfaction. He studied me and I did my best not to squirm under his examination. "As I'm sure you already heard I've secured one of the spots in the finals."

I hadn't, but it didn't surprise me. I'd come into this assuming he'd make it there. This whole tournament was meant to be a big celebration of his impending coronation. "Well, from what I hear it's been a pretty easy tournament for you. I mean, no one wants to be that person who knocks the Crown Prince out early."

"No, I suppose not. But I've got my eye on you." He turned his head toward Talia. "But of course, I don't expect to see you after tomorrow's match."

"Thanks for the ringing endorsement." I gripped the fork tighter to keep from punching him in the face. "Don't you have some coronation preparations to attend to?"

He smirked. "Not that I want to agree with you, but yes, I do."

He stood, drawing everyone's attention again as he left the room. Only once the doors had shut behind him did I let up my grip on the utensil. "He's trying to intimidate me."

"He's worried."

"That's him worried?"

"Yes, because he knows you stand a real chance of beating him," Gethin said.

Now more than ever I needed to decompress with Julayne. She'd have some pearls of wisdom for me. Or at the very least she'd trash talk Arthur with me. "I need to get some air."

I left Gethin behind and made my way to the courtyard. I gave the stone where Excalibur sat a wide berth. Even at this distance, I could still feel its pull. I paced back and forth, wearing a path in the dirt beneath my feet. I felt a presence come up behind me and my body tensed. I spun to find Shunae standing behind me. She wore casual clothes and sported dark sunglasses. It reminded me just how much Camelot and London were alike. When I wasn't fighting to reclaim my life, I'd have to go exploring and figure out just how similar the two places were.

"Walk with me." She grabbed my arm and dragged me back toward the courtyard's exterior wall.

"What are you doing?" I demanded.

She shoved me up against the stone and held out her hand, tilting the glasses down so she could make eye contact. "Shake my hand."

"What?" I could hear Emerys' disapproving voice in the back of my head. I had to be careful. I shouldn't trust this woman.

She gave me an exaggerated eye roll, grabbed my hand, and palmed what felt like a slip of paper. When she pulled away, I looked to find a note in my hand.

"Your friend isn't exactly stealthy in his inquiries," she said.

"Were you following him?"

She gave a noncommittal shrug. "I might not be as important or as powerful as his Royal Highness, but I've got friends in high places. Some low ones, too. Look, the person he found is shady as Hell. If you need technology, go there instead. They're cheaper and far more discreet."

"Thanks. You really didn't have to do this."

"You've got potential, Morgan. And something

tells me that you're the kind of person I'm going to want as a friend in the future."

I stood there in the courtyard staring at her, trying to process her words. Did she know who I was? "Uh, thanks. I think."

"Damn girl, learn to take a compliment."

"Sorry. Not exactly the best at that."

"You'll learn," she said with a smile and pointed to my hand. "Might want to move on that sooner than later."

With that, she pushed her glasses up her nose and sauntered back the way she'd come. Once I was certainly alone, I looked down at the slip of paper with an address scribbled on it.

"You can't just run off like that," Gethin called, approaching me at a jog.

"Didn't realize my movements were restricted," I retorted, trying to conceal the paper in my hand.

He snatched it before I had a chance to pocket it. "Where'd you get this?"

"A friend, I think," I answered. "Shunae. She saw you poking around and said this person can get me what I need much cheaper. But seeing as I don't have a clue where to go, and the one thing I'd use to find it is the thing I need help with ... I guess, you and I are going on a mini tour of Camelot."

I EXPECTED the address to be in some sketchy back alley. It turned out to be a simple storefront about a twenty-minute walk from the castle grounds on a high street filled with coffee shops and gift stores. Gethin kept glancing over his shoulder after every street we turned down, even though he'd cast the same spell he'd used to get us off and on the train back to the cabin.

"Would you relax. It's not like I'm looking to buy drugs. Just get my phone working again," I reminded him as I pushed open the door.

"No one would buy that here," he muttered, at least tacitly acknowledging he knew what drugs were.

Tech whirred on shelves all around us. Overhead lights illuminated a path back to a low counter. A lone figure stood with their back to the counter as we approached.

"Just a moment," a male voice said. The figure turned to reveal a middle-aged man with half-moon glasses balanced upon the bridge of his nose. HIs appearance was exactly as I would have pegged an old wizard to look. "How can I help you?"

"Uh, well, I've got a problem with my phone and I heard you might be able to help."

"Technology is my business."

I handed over my phone. He poked at it, pressing the home and power buttons. He cocked his head to one side and said, "Not sure I've seen one quite this out of power."

"I was hoping someone might be able to ... uh, jumpstart it. None of the cables I've got will do the trick."

He set the phone down on the counter between us. "Probably because they weren't made for this type of phone. Guessing you picked this up second-hand. Things slip through sometimes."

"Can you help?"

"Sure, sure."

Relief flooded me. "She's got a bit of a data plan problem, too," Gethin said. "That whole second-hand issue."

The man behind the counter stroked his chin. "Ah, you'd be the lass I'd heard might be coming around."

"Maybe? Depends on who you heard it from." I said with a tight-lipped smile.

"Miss DeVoe is an old client of mine and she

mentioned I might be getting a visit from someone looking for some specific technology magic."

"So, can you help?"

"Don't get many requests like this," he said. "It's doable, just, finnicky."

"I appreciate anything you can do."

He disappeared with my phone through a dark brown curtain, leaving Gethin and I to stand waiting expectantly. "See, this isn't so bad," I told my friend.

"It just feels risky. I didn't want to tell you earlier, but I asked Emerys about this guy and she didn't recommend it. Then again, she didn't recommend any of the guys I found to do what you wanted."

"It's just a phone call," I said as the man returned.

"Right, see if this works," he said, passing it back to me.

I pressed the power button and it came to life, loading my lock screen—a photo of Aunt Nim, Julayne, and I from New Year's a year ago. To my surprise, the battery was full.

"This was dead literally a minute ago," I remarked.

"Magic's grand, isn't it? Now, the calling range is limited I'm afraid. That sort of plan is rather expensive and I have a feeling you were looking to keep this as low-cost as possible."

If I could make one call to Julayne, I'd be fine. "Yeah, that's fine. How much is it?"

He pointed to my face. "You're in the tournament. Facing Princess Talia tomorrow."

"Uh, yeah. That's me."

"I'll make you a deal. You make it to the finals and I'll waive the fee."

"Why would you do that?" Gethin piped up.

I waved off his question. "That's very generous of you," I began but Gethin cut me off.

"If we're doing this, we are paying you for your service," He said, his tone firm.

"Well, if you insist."

Gethin handed over a card and the man fiddled with what looked like an antiquated till. He handed back the card and a receipt. Gethin didn't even bother looking at the total as we left the shop.

"I'm going to make this call. I'll see you back at the room," I said once we were back on the castle grounds.

"Don't go far," he called as he retreated to the room.

I followed him at a slower pace, studying the

image of my friend and aunt on my phone. "You'd both be proud of me," I whispered.

I expected to see a barrage of missed calls and texts from Julayne. But I only had a couple of texts and no missed calls. Maybe they hadn't gotten through.

The first text was from the day after Emerys and I had left London.

> Hope you made it to where you
> were going.

Then another came two days ago.

> Missing you, love. Things have
> been too quiet without you.

I opened my contacts and dialed Julayne's number. My heart hammered in my throat as I listened to the line ring. *It actually worked!* The line kept ringing with no answer. Then, Julayne's voice-mail kicked on and hearing her voice brought tears to my eyes.

"Hey, Jules, it's me. I'm sorry I haven't responded to your texts. Only just got them. Things are a bit weird around here. But it's so much like Aunt Nim said it would be. And so different, too. God, there's so much I want to share with you. I could really use my best friend right now. I never wanted to do any of this without you. I'm sorry I didn't bring you along. If I could go back to that night, I would have insisted you come with me. You're as much a part of all this as I am."

I began to pace the length of the balcony in front of the door to the room I shared with Gethin.

"I know this is going to cut me off in a minute, but I just wanted to say that I miss you, too. Oh, and you'd appreciate just how bloody good-looking all the blokes are here. Anyway, I don't know if I'll be able to call again. Magic and technology don't mix so well, but I promise I will come see you when this is over."

I ended the call and stowed my phone. The sun had long ago descended past the horizon. The sky was a beautiful shade of navy and deep purple. I marveled at how bright the stars were overhead. Somehow the people of Camelot had managed to create a modern city without all of the light pollution I was accustomed to back home. In the stillness of the moment, I could almost believe that this was home. I could almost picture my place among these people. They weren't ready to fully embrace me yet, but hoped I had time to make it happen.

SIXTEEN

I woke with far more energy than I'd expected the day of my match against Talia. Even though I hadn't been able to talk to Julayne, just hearing her voicemail message had been enough to help me focus. I'd risen early and found some footage of Talia's previous matches, including ones from the current tournament. She made wielding magic look effortless and graceful like a dance. I got lost in the way her body flowed from one place to the next. She never transformed, yet I could swear she floated through the air.

Finding a way to keep her grounded appeared to be my best approach. I noticed she used eye contact to direct a lot of her magic. Perhaps blinding her wasn't a bad option either.

"You look to be in a better mood," Emerys said, appearing on the balcony. I was already dressed in my uniform, waiting for the referee to come collect us.

"I guess I am," I said. "Sleep will do that for a person."

"Gethin told me about your call to your friend. I trust he made my disagreement with that plan known? You could have been followed or the call intercepted."

"It wasn't really a call. She didn't answer. I left a message. But it was nice to hear her voice even for just a few seconds on the recording."

"Having lifted spirits is a good way to approach this match. I shouldn't have to remind you there is a lot riding on the outcome."

"I get it. You want to come home ..." I said.

"I also heard that Prince Arthur has bet against you, yet again. It appears he lost quite a large sum on the last match."

"Do you think the people of Camelot know he's a shit gambler?" I said with a laugh.

"Even with his faults, he is well-liked by Camelot and its neighbors too. Which is all the more reason to get them on your side."

"Believe me, I've been trying."

Just then, the referee—the same woman who'd called my match against Gunter—appeared, waving me down the steps. Emerys trailed me and I spotted Gethin hurrying out of the room as I reached the ground level. I expected the referee to lead us to one of the farther pitches, but she brought us to the pitch directly beyond the courtyard. The stands were packed with people. I even noticed some people in the higher tiers standing crammed together. The energy in the place was far more collegial than either of my other matches had been. I walked to the center of the pitch and shook hands with Talia.

"Good luck," she said. "I have a good feeling about this match."

"Thanks. You, too."

The referee stepped out of range, blew the trumpet twice and bellowed, "Begin." I watched as Talia's torso undulated inward and she blew out a breath of flame that coalesced into her hand. It was impressive except for the fact she was about to send it hurtling in my direction.

I threw up a hand to block the anticipated attack and the opaque shield I'd used against Gunter materialized with far less effort than I'd needed last time. Talia cocked her head to one side, studying my shield before she flung the fireball off to my left. That seemed odd until I felt the heat on my back as it shot around on a curved trajectory.

"One hit, Princess Talia," the referee called.

Fire danced along her arms and she began to do a dramatic pirouette, sending tiny flames shooting skyward. They bounced around in all directions. She was showing off and the crowd cheered at her natural showmanship. I imagined the shield on my arm elongating into more of a bat and gripped it, trying my best to smack the flames back at Talia. I landed a couple of good hits, but she'd caught me from behind, too. They came too fast for me to register until the referee called the score.

"One point, Princess Talia. Two hits, Miss le Fey."

I observed that Talia always pushed off the ground with her left foot. If I could keep her immobilized even for just a few seconds, I could at least even the score. I crouched, pressing my palm to the ground. I felt tiny shoots of grass spring up at my touch. They rippled across the ground to ensnare Talia's foot, winding its way up her leg until it reached the patch on her left thigh that would register the hit. The grass crackled with energy—just enough to even the score.

"One point all."

Talia waved her hand and the grass wilted, withering away to nothing. She flashed a smile before jogging away from me. I stood up just as she took a running leap into the air, arms outspread. In mid-air, she transformed. Even her uniform shifted to accommodate the increase in size and the addition of wings and a tail. Thick bronze plated armor rippled along her body and I could swear she was still smiling at me even with a mouth full of sharp teeth. The crowd let out a collective gasp as she did a circle around the stands. I flashed back to the qualifying trial where the large dragon-shaped form had appeared overhead. I couldn't just run away from it here. There was nowhere to go. I was wholly exposed where I stood and if I didn't do *something* fast I knew she'd land enough hits to end the match in a matter of minutes. She kept circling overhead and I took off at a run toward her side of the pitch. I turned and spotted Taron standing in her entourage box. His presence caught me off guard. So much so that Talia landed a hit to my back yet again.

He looked just as surprised as I did by the move and made a gesture that meant I should turn around. I spun on my heel and stared down the massive creature hovering in the sky overhead.

There was no way I'd win in an airborne fight. She had every advantage, not least of which being she was literally born to fly. But something in the back of my mind whispered the fact she always appeared to make deliberate eye contact with wherever she was directing her magic.

I threw my hands up and pulled them across my body as if I were drawing curtains. Each time it got easier to summon the fog and my eyes adjusted to their enhanced state I now associated with the spell. Unfortunately, it lasted only a few seconds before Talia opened her mouth and blew a stream of fire straight at me, burning through the fog as it went. It hit the ground only a few paces shy of my left foot.

Well fog wasn't the answer, but that didn't mean she was impervious to all types of weather. Even the best pilots hated to fly through thunderstorms.

Make it rain.

The droplets were small at first and they barely even hit my face. But I released my grip on my power, turning the firehose on full blast. The skies opened and rain pummeled my opponent. Thunder boomed overhead and lightning split the sky. Talia did a few barrel rolls to try and avoid the strikes, but a few made contact with patches of her uniform.

"Two points to one, Mis le Fey," the referee called out amidst the deluge.

Talia dropped to the ground, doing an awkward roll as she shifted back to human form. On the ground, the weather didn't seem to be much of a deterrent for her. She held her hands out in front of her. Violent gusts of wind whipped in my direction, turning the storm back on me.

In a panic, I tried to tamp down on my power and make the storm recede. It took a long few seconds, but it finally faded. The rain had soaked me through and matted my hair to my head. I should have thought about that before I'd just altered the weather. For her part, Talia's body gave out trails of steam as she dried herself just like I'd seen Taron do the day we'd met. Behind Talia, I spotted him give me what I took as an encouraging nod. It only served to confuse me though. He should be rooting for Talia since he was here with her after all.

Talia shook her hands at her sides, but didn't attempt to make another move. That meant I had time to catalog the information I now had learned about my opponent. She was comfortable shifting between forms, although I was fairly certain the shift to dragon form had been more to entertain the crowd than a tactical move. She could easily produce fire and wind. Based on that I suspected cold wasn't her favorite thing.

Speaking of cold, I shivered in the dampness. Maybe I could work with that. I tried to pull the damp and the chill out of my own body, forcing it to pool in my hands like dry ice. It smoked and frothed against my fingers. By the time it covered my fore-arms I was feeling much less miserable. I turned my hands, palms out and directed the smoky magic toward Talia's extremities. It shot across the space between us and wrapped around her hands and moved up her arms, locking her body in a frozen state.

I knew it wouldn't hold her for long, so I took my shot. I funneled my power into a single shining sphere in front of me. I needed two more points to win. I tried to divide the sphere into six smaller ones, but had only managed to split it once before I noticed the frost on Talia's hands begin to melt away.

So much for the quick and dirty route.

I sent the two spheres at her. The first one went for a direct hit. It landed against her chest. She took a staggering step backwards. The second one I did my best to put as much spin on it as I could, taking a page from her book. It zipped around her, stopped in mid-air, and then went zooming to strike the plate on her back. The ice had crept far enough up her arms for it to trigger the patch on her left elbow.

"Three points to two, Miss le Fey."

Only three more hits and this match would be over. As they went, it hadn't been that taxing or bloody. I appreciated that she didn't try to strangle me, or light me on fire, or even eat me. The last bits of ice had melted and a series of rapid-fire globs of energy came at me. I dove to the ground to avoid them, but one still grazed my knee. It wasn't an official hit per the rules, but it was enough to burn a hole in the material and leave an angry red mark on my skin.

So much for coming out of this unscathed. Even with her barrage of fire balls, Talia still appeared to move slowly and she was favoring her left shoulder. Perhaps her sudden landing had done some damage after all. I pushed myself to my feet and felt her weight collide with mine, taking me back to the ground. She pinned me, her full weight settling over my torso. I expected her to land enough blows to at least even the score, but she didn't.

I shoved her off, purposely sending her onto her bad shoulder. I heard her hiss in pain as she skittered in the dirt. I scrambled to my feet, waiting for her next move.

When Talia got to her feet, her eyes glowed with an eerie orange glint, as if the fire inside of her was going to come out as lasers. In that moment, I hated that the uniforms didn't come with extra fabric. A blindfold or sunglasses would be handy.

Talia's body bent inward as she prepared to cough up another ball of flame. I was running out of time to act. I flung my hand out, pouring power into the gesture. I envisioned her eyes going milky and she let out a shriek. Pale opaque lenses replaced the vibrant orange. She couldn't see.

Please let it be only temporary.

Even though she couldn't see, she still flung fire in every direction. Most landed harmlessly in the dirt. I could see her shutting her eyes tight, like she thought she could burn the magic away. The next time she started flinging fire, I was ready. The shield I'd first conjured rematerialized and deflected her attacks. In short order, three had struck her and the match was called for me.

I rushed toward her. "Hold on. I'm going to undo it," I whispered.

"You better not have just blinded me," she hissed back.

I gripped her hands tight in mine and in my mind's eye, I saw the milkiness vanish, replaced by her regular irises. Lime filled my nose and when Talia opened her eyes again, they were normal. I heaved a sigh of relief and let her hand go.

"Good match," I said, taking a step back and offering her my hand.

"Good luck taking on Arthur."

The reality that I would now be facing off against Arthur hit me like a ton of bricks. It was what we'd been working toward since I'd arrived in Camelot, but it had always felt just out of reach. Even as I'd marched down to the arena for this match, a tiny part of me believed I wouldn't make it. And yet, here I was, set to face him in two days' time. Gethin rushed me on the pitch and threw his arms around me.

"You did it. I knew you would," he praised.

"It's really happening," I said as he ushered me off the pitch.

"People are going to be talking about this match for ages. I mean, I told you no one ever shifts during the tournament. But she did, and you still managed to take her down. She could have roasted you!" Gethin chattered excitedly as we left the pitch behind.

"Glad we could put on a good show," I said as the ambient noise of the crowd began to fade.

"You did well," Emerys said, emerging from the shadows of the grounds. "You are so very close to the end now."

We headed back to the lodging area and as I started up the stairs to our room, I spotted Arthur. The look of fury on his face was evident even from this distance. He knew we would be facing one another in the final match. Not to mention I'd cost him money twice already. With my win, he was now poised to lose even more. He wasn't going to make it easy on me.

This tournament hadn't managed to kill me, yet. But with the way he was glaring at me, there was a very real chance he was going to try to change that before all of this was over.

SEVENTEEN

It barely felt like I had time to catch my breath from the semi-finals match against Talia before going into the final round against Arthur. My head was still spinning with the fact I'd actually beaten a *dragon*. As had become my ritual, I snuck from the room and made my way down to the grounds at sunrise. This was the first time I'd made the trek alone.

Unlike other mornings I'd taken the route past the courtyard along the castle's outer walls. This time there weren't workers feverishly setting up for the day's events. Everyone had today off to rest and I suspected some of the eliminated participants were heading home. They might want to watch the match tomorrow, but they could do that from the comfort of their own homes. As I trailed my hand along the rough stonework of the castle wall, I heard footsteps behind me. Momentary fear turned my legs to stone.

"Seems we don't need a lake for an early morning rendezvous," a familiar voice called. Taron appeared in my peripheral vision and I relaxed. "Although I admit to being less prone to running about naked in public."

I laughed at his remark, immediately conjuring that image of him emerging from the water for the first time. It sent warmth coursing through my body. I waited for him to stop beside me before speaking. "Their loss."

Taron laughed, his teeth gleaming in the early morning light. "We don't need that scandal, trust me."

"I was surprised to see you at the match yesterday."

"Well, I couldn't not support my little sister."

His words slowly registered in my head. Talia was his sister. But she'd been announced as the Dragon's crown princess. That meant she was next in line to inherit the throne in her kingdom. "You're a prince?"

"Unfortunately," he sighed. "Now you know why I can't go streaking through the streets. It would cause a diplomatic incident and no one needs that headache."

"Sorry, I'm just a little confused. I thought Talia's the next in line for the Dragon throne?"

"She is."

"But she's younger than you."

He cocked his head to one side. "Yes. Where's the confusion?"

"But doesn't succession go by who is oldest?"

"Ah ... Technically, yes. Until I was eighteen, I was the crown prince. But I wasn't ever meant to lead. At least not an entire kingdom."

"I know that feeling."

"It wasn't even just a feeling. I saw the way my sister was with people. The way she could command a room even as a young girl. I knew that we needed her in power one day. Maybe I'm a bit selfish. But I didn't want that to happen just because I'd died and left behind no children. So, I petitioned my father to allow me to abdicate, to renounce my claim to the crown in favor of Talia."

"And she was okay with that?"

"Don't worry, I'm not giving her anything she isn't ready for."

"I don't know many people who'd give up that kind of prestige."

"I suppose I'm not most people," he retorted.

I stopped myself from blurting out, 'No you're not.'

"So, I suppose you're rather disappointed your sister didn't make it to the finals?" I said, beginning to walk again. He fell into step beside me, hands hanging loosely at his sides.

"Actually, I've been following you since the first round." He grinned at me. "When you mentioned you were entering, I was intrigued."

Embarrassment warmed the nape of my neck. I could feel it creeping to my cheeks and the tips of my ears. "You're the first person who has said they're a fan. Well, besides my mate who's kind of my trainer and this little girl named Tillie I met at the train station."

"You have some really creative approaches. I thought you were very impressive. And it made the tournament interesting again. It's been dull for ages."

"I watched footage of the final match from last year. It was close," I noted.

"No one doubted that Arthur would win. He always wins when it's on his home court."

Without realizing it, he'd answered a question that had lingered in the back of mind all week. The tournament traveled. It made sense. That way no specific kingdom felt they always had the upper hand. It also made me smile knowing Arthur didn't always have it so easy.

"You make it seem like I've had some grand plan going into this. I haven't. I've just been winging it. Trying things and seeing what works."

"Well, keep it up, because it's clearly a winning strategy."

We reached a gated area and turned around the way we'd come in unison. We made our way back to the courtyard. I stopped short of going inside as the magical pull of Excalibur wrapped around me, trying to lure me in. I dug my heels in and pressed my right hand against the stonework beside me to try and keep myself immobile. The longer I spent here, the stronger its pull had become.

"What's wrong?" Taron's tone was all concern and when I managed to look into his eyes, all I saw was genuine worry.

In that moment, I wanted to tell him everything; the truth about who I was and what I was here to do. But Emerys was so distrusting of anyone besides Gethin that I wasn't sure what she'd do if I brought Taron in on the secret. Except it pained me to lie to him. We barely knew each other, but my intuition told me he was someone I should lean on.

"It's ... nothing. I just need to hydrate or get something to eat. I haven't been good about that the last few days," I said, hating every word that came out of my mouth.

"You need to keep your strength up," he said, looping an arm around my shoulders and guiding me away from the wall.

Mercifully, he led me back to the lodging area and the communal dining room. He sat me down and disappeared out of view. I rested my head on my forearms and took a few steadying breaths. The pull of the sword had lessened, but it was only a temporary reprieve. Tomorrow, I would face Arthur in that very same courtyard and there'd be no escaping the sword's influence.

When Taron returned, he carried two plates, heaped with eggs, bread, and a fresh orange on one plate, and what looked like a peach in its place on the other. "Wasn't sure what you'd want so I got a bit of everything."

I'd been spoiled by Gethin insisting on making me breakfast every morning, but I greedily accepted the plate with the orange and tucked in. "I'm surprised you don't get mobbed more by the crowd," I said around a bite of food. "Being royalty and all."

"There aren't many people clamoring for an autograph of the guy who was supposed to be King."

"I don't know, I'd fancy one," I quipped and then took a bite of eggs.

"For you, I'd make an exception," he said with a laugh. "So long as I got one in return."

"But I'm nobody," I mumbled.

"Nonsense. You're the woman who is going to beat that pompous prick at his own game and claim the victor's trophy," he retorted.

"Everyone seems so convinced I'm going to win this thing. But he's got loads more experience than I do. For one thing, he's actually won the tournament before. My magic's erratic at best." I hadn't meant for the last bit to slip out, but there was no putting that particular cat back in the proverbial bag.

"Performance anxiety?" he suggested.

"Uh, not exactly. For a long time the connection to my magic didn't work right. It's better now, but I still have trouble controlling it."

"Well, you hide it masterfully," he whispered.

The conversation died down as other participants emerged from their rooms with their entourages. I spotted Talia. She came down the stairs and made eye contact with Taron before disappearing in the direction of the buffet. When she returned with a plate of food and made a direct path for our table, I wanted to run.

But my legs refused to follow my brain's directive.

"What's going on here?" She addressed Taron.

"Just sharing a meal with a new friend," he countered.

"I met her first," Talia noted, as if laying claim to my attention.

"Actually, we met before the tournament even started," Taron boasted. "At the lake during one of my morning swims."

Talia turned to me. "So, you've seen my brother in all of his glory and haven't gone screaming for the hills. I knew you were made of tough stuff."

"It was an accident." Well, at least the first time.

"You're making her uncomfortable, Tal," Taron chided. "And Morgan doesn't need that sort of distraction if she's going to beat Arthur tomorrow."

"You've become something of an underdog in this competition," Talia said. "You've got my support. If I'm being honest, I may have given you a few extra openings yesterday to get through."

"You cheated?" I coughed.

"No. You won fair and square, but a couple of my choices just made it a little easier for you to do so. Don't worry, we'll both be cheering you on from the stands."

"Thanks." After a moment, I added, "I probably ought to go find my friend. He'll want to do some last minute training exercises before tomorrow."

Taron was on his feet, offering me a hand up. It wasn't necessary, but I appreciated the gesture. Across the table I heard Talia fake-cough in her hand, saying something about him being a flirt.

"Thanks for breakfast," I told him, looking at a spot just off his right shoulder. If I looked him in the eyes, I might just sit back down and never leave.

"When all of this is over, I hope we'll see each other again." He leaned in close, his lips mere centimeters from my ear and whispered, "Perhaps for an early morning swim ... together."

A shiver that had nothing to do with being cold wriggled through my core at his words. I made a show of gathering my empty plate and disposing of it before heading back to the room I'd shared with Gethin for the last week. The door opened inward before I could reach for the handle.

"Where have you been?" Gethin demanded.

Frown lines accentuated by the lenses of his glasses signaled he'd been worried about me.

"I'm fine. Just went for a walk and had a bite to eat. I was coming to find you to do some training and strategizing for tomorrow."

"You shouldn't be going out alone, especially now when you're so close to the finals," he said, ushering me inside.

"Relax, no one actually knows who I am. It's not like anyone's going to come try and assassinate me."

"I wouldn't be so sure. You were attacked by Seelie soldiers in your world, remember? They didn't just happen to show up there by accident."

"Yeah, but we haven't heard anything from them since we got here." I didn't remind him how I thought I'd seen one of the soldiers during my match against Gunter.

"Someone's bound to know they failed their mission to kill you. And now that you've made it to the finals, we can't take any chances. Besides, Arthur doesn't always play fair."

"He might not fight fair, but I have to believe if he thinks he's about to be King, he wants to keep the people on his side. He doesn't want to come off as a cheating prick in front of everyone."

"Maybe not, but that doesn't mean you're safe."

I sunk onto the edge of the bed nearest the door and let his words sink in. I'd been so focused on the tournament and not getting eliminated, I'd completely forgotten the men who'd murdered my Aunt Nim and nearly succeeded in offing me, too until the match with Gunter where I could have sworn I saw one of them. It raised a new question in my mind though. *Why hadn't they tried again?*

"Is that why Emerys hasn't been around? She's not really worried someone will spot her. She's just trying to keep me safe."

"It's a little of both, honestly. She knew those soldiers would eventually get through the barrier back here. And Seelie soldiers are nothing if not determined to follow orders."

For a moment, I felt the phantom grasp of the man's hands around my throat, squeezing the life out of me. But they hadn't found me, even with the notoriety I'd gained making it to the finals of the tournament. "You don't think they're going to try something at the final match do you?"

"We have to be ready for anything. I'm not convinced Gunter wasn't working with them. I recall you said you thought you saw one of those soldiers during your match with him."

"I said I wasn't sure. It's not like I got up close

and personal with the wanker's entourage." At the time, I'd tried to brush it off as my mind playing tricks, but maybe there'd been more to it than I'd realized.

He paced the distance between the end of the bed and the wall. "You're too important to this kingdom to be allowed to roam free. I know it sounds controlling and archaic, but it's the truth."

"Is that why you freaked out before we came here when I was alone at the lake?"

He straightened his glasses. "I didn't freak out."

"You totally did, mate. Though, I suppose that was probably more from who I was talking to." The look of confusion on his face made me smirk. "I know he's royalty. Or I do now anyhow. But I guess I can see why you'd be worried about me talking to him."

"Historically, the dragons have been our allies. But you can never be too safe."

"Well, you can relax, because I haven't told Taron anything about who I really am."

"Oh, you're on a first name basis with him, are you?"

I grabbed the nearest pillow and lobbed it at him, hitting him in the chest. "Don't be jealous."

He threw the pillow back at me and offered a

smile. "I'm not jealous, Okay, maybe a little, but can you blame me? He's a dragon!" That broke the tension in the room as we both fell into fits of laughter. I toppled back on the bed and he laid down beside me, discarding his glasses so he could wipe the tears from his eyes. We laid side by side for a few moments in companionable silence and I watched him. The stress lines on his face had receded some, replaced by laugh lines. And he had a smile on his lips, even though he kept trying to hide it.

"Has anyone ever stopped to think how absolutely stupid this tournament is? I mean, you send your best people to essentially fight to the death with magic for fun. It's madness. And for a kingdom run by women for hundreds of years, it seems oddly destructive."

"Sometimes I forget how not normal all of this is for you," he sighed. "The way we do things, I mean. It's got to be a huge culture shock."

"To be honest, I'm used to blokes being dicks to me on a daily basis. I'm just not used to them trying to kill me just because I exist." I rolled onto my side to face him. "I guess since I haven't ever really considered myself a princess even as a kid, the thought of that being the case still feels unreal to me."

"After tomorrow, everyone's going to know who you really are and if they come after you, it will be an act of war. And no one actually wants that."

"That still assumes I beat Arthur. I meant what I said earlier. I was coming to find you to strategize and train. I'm going to need all the practice I can get."

EIGHTEEN

My nerves had been in my throat all morning as I prepared to walk into the central courtyard of the castle to face Arthur. There were moments I still couldn't believe I'd gotten here on my own merit. Every match leading to this point had been grueling and yet I'd somehow come out on the other side the victor.

"Your worry is palpable," Emerys said softly as she came to stand at my side staring outward as workers made final preparations for the match.

Somehow they'd transferred all of the seating from the makeshift pitches on the grounds to fill the space of the courtyard overnight. I was also fairly certain they'd expanded the size of the courtyard, too. Logically, part of me recognized they'd used magic, but that still didn't make the awe of the feat disappear.

I'd seen crowds already gathering at the gates as early as six in the morning even though our round wasn't set to start until noon. The signs sporting my name had warmed my heart a little, but as the reality ticked closer that I was facing the Camelot's Crown Prince—the man I'd been told had stolen my crown—the more my fear reared its ugly head.

"Can you blame me that I'm bloody terrified?" I finally said.

"You have come so far in such a short time. This is everything we've worked for."

"Most of that was luck. And no one even knows who I truly am. So, even if I do beat him, and let's be honest, that's still a really big if ... who's going to believe me if I just pop up after it's all over and say, 'Oh, by the way, I'm the real heir.'"

"You need to believe that your true identity will be made known at the right moment."

I wanted to tell her I was getting really tired of her cryptic pep talks. I looked around, hoping to spot Gethin, but he was nowhere to be seen. I didn't want to head into the arena without my friend there to cheer me on. He'd been integral to getting me this far.

"Where's Gethin? He wouldn't miss this, right?"

"He's just doing a bit of reconnaissance," Emerys answered. "Now, let's get you ready. You've only just a little more to go, Morgan."

I swallowed back my nerves and we headed for the changing area. As I tugged my hair out of my face and braided it close to my neck I heard the chanting and cheers of the crowd as they assembled. Looking in the mirror, I imagined I was talking to Aunt Nim.

"I'm really trying to believe you prepared me for this, Aunt Nim. I want to honor you and make you proud. I love you."

'I love you too, my pretty girl.'

I turned, swearing I could hear her voice whispering in my ear. For a brief moment, my reflection had vanished, replaced by her smiling face. But then I blinked and she was gone. The voice had faded too. Still I clung to the belief that in some small way, she was here with me now.

Before I knew it, the referee came to escort me to the courtyard. Bodies filled every seat in the stands and I could see large screens broadcasting the event for those not lucky enough to secure live access. I could see the Queen sitting in a separate box at the far end of the pitch. I spotted a similar box on the other side where a tall, slender man sat with a bronze crown perched neatly on his head. I waited for the cameras to pan over him, enlarging his image on the screens to confirm that his ears indeed sloped to a point. The pin on his collar identified him as fae. He turned as the camera panned over him. I could swear he made eye contact with me and a shiver danced down my spine.

The feeling subsided, replaced by something equally as unnerving—the pull of the sword wedged in stone in the center of the courtyard. I'd done my best to avoid the space until now. Emerys had explained that the sword, while not sentient, was imbued with so much magic and the blood of my ancestors, it couldn't help but call out to me. It was like a siren song, drawing every bit of my focus.

"Just what I don't need," I muttered under my breath.

Maybe if I put my back to the blasted thing, it wouldn't be quite so distracting. I moved to the center of the courtyard and positioned myself so the stone was to my back. Arthur strolled out from the other side of the stands, looking confident and fresh-faced. Gethin had urged me to watch the high-lights of Arthur's other matches from the tourna-ment, but I'd been too exhausted to absorb much of what I'd seen. From what had stuck in my mind, he hadn't been challenged much at all in any of the rounds he'd gone through. No one wanted to be the one to knock the prince out of the tournament, especially in Camelot.

The stadium erupted with cheers at his arrival and he gave a diplomatic wave to the assembled crowd as he approached me. The referee followed after him. Arthur gave me a sugary fake smile.

"I have to admit, you came out of nowhere and have put up quite the fight to get here. But you don't belong here little girl," he said, spitting those last words. His lips were still plastered into a smile, holding his handsome facade.

"Hate to break it to you, but I played by the rules. I've every right to be here." I stopped short of telling him that the crown he was about to claim wasn't really his.

"Everyone here wants to see me win. It's what they expect," he continued. "And I have to give the people what they want after all."

The referee reached between us before I could point out the slew of signs with my name on them. I tuned Arthur out as the official told us not to shed too much blood. I'd learned quickly that blood was part of this sport. Camelot might be populated with dragons, fae, and humans, but they were far more brutal than anyone I'd ever encountered in London.

The shrill echo of the trumpet announcing the start of the match rang painfully in my ears. It could have been my imagination, but the crowd grew silent as they waited for one of us to make the first move. As Arthur raised his arms, all of the knowledge I'd amassed in the last week fled my mind. It was as if I'd never used magic in my life. I didn't even try to dodge the blast of energy he hurtled at me.

His power slammed into my chest, knocking me back a few paces. My uniform sensors lit up, signaling he'd earned the first hit of the match before crackling along my limbs, pinning my arms to my sides. Panic gripped my throat tight enough to stop the intake of breath.

I vaguely felt his power wrap tight around my legs. A moment later, I stared up at the clear blue sky overhead from where I'd toppled onto my back. I heard a smattering of boos go up around me, but even that wasn't enough to free myself from the sudden brain fog. I struggled pointlessly against the power restricting my every movement and I heard Arthur let out a laugh. There was a harshness I hadn't picked up on before in his tone.

"I know I said you don't belong here, but come on … don't make this boring," he taunted, leaning over me with a web of violet-colored magic dancing along his palm, ready to strike.

"One hit to zero, Prince Arthur," the referee's voice boomed.

In that moment, his features shifted. Part of my oxygen-starved brain wanted to claim it was a trick of light, but I knew better. The way the angles of his face sharpened along his jawline and nose, and the way the tip of his left ear shimmered to reveal a point told me he was concealing his true identity with magic.

I glanced to my right. The sword still sat firmly encased in stone, but I willed it to call out to me and give my addled brain something else to focus on. It resonated in my head like an impact hammer. I focused on the vibrations as they ran down my body. I pictured them snipping the bindings of his magic as they went and after a moment, I could move of my own accord again. Reacquainting my body with the concept of breathing took a moment, but the burning in my lungs subsided.

"Must be exhausting being you," I finally managed through a cough.

I flexed my fingers and envisioned the ground

beneath me bending to my will, buoying me back to my feet. Sand, gravel, and tiny blades of grass leapt to attention, eager to help me. I watched Arthur's expression change, his eyes widened with shock.

"Oh, and your mask is slipping … Your Highness," I said, gesturing to his face.

His shock melted into rage as he let the magic loose from his hands. Something had shifted within me, too and I held up my right hand. The scent of lime swirled around me, so strong it made my lips pucker from the sourness. I embraced it, letting it wrap around me like armor.

Time appeared to slow as the energy hurtled toward me. Without realizing I'd put the intent out into the world, the magic touched the tips of my fingers. Instead of deflecting back on my opponent, they turned an iridescent green before it skittered up my arm and settled in my chest.

Did I just absorb his magic?

The bit of magic that now hovered within my breastbone suggested I had in fact taken on his power. I'd never known that was possible. Even as I stood with him staring at me in disbelief, the power began to rebel against me. It wanted to be returned to where it came from.

Fine by me.

I pulled my right hand back as if to strike him in the face and let the magic slither down my arm, ramping up velocity as it did so. I swung wide, not intending to actually hit Arthur, but the magic flew off me, colliding with his face and radiating down far enough to make contact with the chest plate on his uniform.

"One hit all," the referee announced.

In front of me, Arthur straightened and waved his hands in an exaggerated gesture. He vanished. A moment later, twenty Arthurs populated the court-yard. Illusions. He was borrowing from the Seelie playbook.

The Arthur nearest to me cupped his hands together before summoning white-hot flames and blew them in my direction. I threw myself to the ground, managing to roll out of the path of the flames. My uniform shimmered pale green, reminding me of the fact I still had a protection spell wrapped around me. It might not have hurt me if it had landed. Still, I didn't want to find out if I could avoid it.

I pushed myself to my feet and pulled the air in around me, picturing the thickest fog I could imagine. By this point, it had become something of a signature move for me. And Arthur had clearly studied my moves. The flames he lobbed missed me, striking the ground, but they were powerful enough to disrupt my cover. Another Arthur began sending bolts of electricity all around me.

I lobbed an energy ball of my own at the nearest shadow. I heard it sizzle as it struck the target. I waited for the referee to call out the change in score, but there was nothing. Apparently hitting one of the illusionary Arthurs didn't' count.

Just as I pivoted to send out another blast, a wave of dirt and grass came crashing down on me. He'd turned the literal ground beneath my feet against me. It knocked the air from my lungs and my head slammed into something sharp. I could swear I heard something crack and tasted blood in the back of my throat.

"Two hits to one, Prince Arthur," the referee announced.

How the fuck was that fair?

His illusions could score against me, but not the other way around. Bullshit.

I needed a better strategy. Flailing about blindly, hoping I hit the real thing, wasn't going to get me any closer to winning this match. I struggled to free myself from the pile of dirt weighing me down. If he could use Seelie illusions to confuse me, there were other options I could use too.

Staggering to my feet, I willed the fog to dissipate. Where there had been twenty Arthurs filling the courtyard moments ago, now there were only nineteen. So, hitting the fakes took them out of play. That was good to know. I needed a different perspective though.

Let me fly.

Almost of its own accord, the air around me took on mass, launching me skyward. I lacked the wings of a dragon, but the power I'd pulled from the world around me was enough to keep me aloft. Shifting my position above my opponent was exactly what I'd needed. I could see the Arthur who'd been farthest from me appeared to be standing still in a trancelike state. Getting the other imposters off the field would help, but if he was focused on controlling his puppets, he wouldn't see me coming.

The distance between us shrunk as I hurtled toward him. I reached out, got my fingers into the folds of the fabric around the chest plate and tackled him to the ground. The impact was enough to force his eyes open. All around us, the crowd gasped. In my peripheral vision the nearest illusions sputtered out of existence.

I shifted my weight enough to be able to strike his chest plate twice.

"One point to Miss le Fey," the referee announced, a hint of surprise coloring his voice.

One down. Three more to go.

***

THE SUN WAS BEGINNING its descent as the afternoon turned to evening. Apart from a short twenty-minute break, Arthur and I had been at it for the last five hours, trading hits. Somehow, we were tied at three points each. Much like what had happened in my very first match with Shunae.

"I can't keep this up," I said as Gethin forced a cup of water into my shaking hands. Every muscle ached and I'd busted my lip during a particularly nasty fall.

"You only need to make it a little longer. Just three more hits," he said.

"You say that like it's easy," I whined.

"Just do it like you did in your first match. Get behind him and hit fast."

I turned to Emerys, hoping for some guidance. She reached over with a cloth and wiped some of the blood from my face. "Your trial will soon be over. Have faith."

The referee's horn signaled the break was over and I forced myself back onto the pitch. Thankfully, I'd been able to get a few good licks in. Arthur sported some cuts on his arm and a nasty bruise bloomed on his right cheek.

"This ends now," he growled and thrust out a hand in my direction.

As if I were a marionette, my arms and legs were no longer within my control. He yanked me up and spun me around in mid-air before slamming me arm-first into the stone where Excalibur remained encased.

I couldn't stop myself from letting out a pained cry as I felt something snap between my shoulder and elbow. I tried not to look down, but morbid curiosity got the better of me. I could see bone piercing skin and my stomach lurched. My whole body went numb. I barely registered the blows Arthur dealt to my back.

"Two hits to none, Prince Arthur," the referee announced.

One more hit and this would be over. Part of me longed for him to just finish it, so I could rest. A week ago, I'd just been an unknown bartender in

London whose magic didn't work worth a damn. No one expected me to do anything important. Besides, no one would really care if I just went home.

'Free me.'

Excalibur's siren call rang out in my head as if someone had screamed in my ear. I glanced up at the hilt of the sword shining in the dying sunlight, its sapphire encrusted surface glittering and beautiful. I dug my right hand into the nearest crevice in the stone to pull me to my feet. I tried to press my broken arm to my chest to protect it and pain seared through my whole body. I let out another cry. My right hand came away bloody. My fingers shook as I reached for the blade, the rest of the world falling away.

I pressed my hand to the hilt and it illuminated in a blinding blue light. A high-pitched ringing filled my ears, intensifying the longer I stood there with my skin against the blade. Unsure of what else to do, I grasped the hilt and pulled.

The sword came free and I stood there in the middle of the courtyard, brandishing Excalibur for the whole Kingdom to see.

NINETEEN

I don't know who was more surprised by the fact I now stood brandishing a sword half the length of my body, me or Arthur. His jaw worked like he was trying to form words, but nothing came out. The intense buzzing that had driven me to grab the hilt subsided the moment I'd freed the blade from the stone. The echoes still rang in my ears though, blocking out all other sounds. I had enough awareness to gauge the crowd's reaction and the unanimous expressions of shock hit home with what I'd done.

The sword should have felt heavy in my hand. After all, I'd never even held one before, let alone one-handed and injured. Yet it was light as air. I swung it in a wide arc in front of me and Arthur skittered back, putting himself at a safe distance.

"There are no weapons …" the referee began before Arthur regained his composure and waved his hand.

I felt the world's magic ebbing toward his outstretched fingers, coalescing into a sword of his own. Even with Excalibur in hand, I was still on the defense. He only needed one more hit to end the match. But the crowd knew something wasn't right now and even those who'd firmly been cheering for him now turned their attention to me. A week ago, hell even an hour ago, that would have terrified me. Now, it gave a sudden hit of adrenaline.

"You're right about one thing," I called, the agony throbbing in my left arm momentarily dulled by the surge of endorphins. "This is going to be over soon."

"Stop this!" The Queen's voice boomed through the courtyard and I looked to see she'd vacated the spectator's box and materialized in the courtyard with us. However, she didn't approach us.

Arthur pivoted to face her. "It will be over in a moment, Mother. Let us finish."

The queen's jaw worked as she tried to formulate a response. As the screens all focused on her, I could see the confusion and panic on her face as she fought to keep a neutral expression. Finally, she allowed the referee to escort her to a safe distance, signaling we could continue. It was the closest I'd been to the woman who'd given me life since the opening ceremony. Part of me wanted that fear in her eyes to be about my safety, but I knew I was just a stranger to her still.

I couldn't let my emotions distract me from the task at hand. There would be time to share in the bizarre mixture of emotions when this bloody tournament was over. I spun the sword one-handed as if I'd done it a million times and steadied my balance for Arthur's attack. He lunged, his conjured blade raised overhead as he slashed down, gripping the hilt with both hands. The sword more than me anticipated his strike and rose to meet him on its own. The blades clanged metal on metal and a ripple of aquamarine energy leapt from Excalibur to the conjured blade. I could feel Arthur's magic pressing in against me and yet it couldn't get past Excalibur.

The sky above us, which had been a vibrant, cloudless blue, darkened with ominous thunderclouds. The shift in air pressure made my ears pop and I felt the tiny hairs on the nape of my neck bristle with the increased electricity in the atmosphere.

"You have no right taking what's mine, bitch!" Arthur snarled, his princely façade dropping just enough to reveal a hunger in his eyes as his gaze settled on the sword in my hand.

The way he tracked the sword's every movement with his gaze signaled he really believed it was meant to be his. In that moment, I couldn't help but wonder how often he'd tried to free it, believing he would one day be worthy of wielding it. He now raised his sword and lightning crackled overhead, striking the metallic blade. Gasps went up from the crowd as they no doubt expected Arthur to wind up with severe burns.

The elements swirled around him as he summoned billowing gusts of wind and a torrent of rain to do his bidding. My fog trick had been just that by comparison. I didn't have true command over the elements, even if my magic was born of this realm.

And yet, I felt the wind and rain trying to land anywhere, but on my body. It was as if the very world around us knew I wasn't meant to come to true harm. If I could find a way to harness that, I could truly put an end to this.

With my injured arm, my options were limited. I couldn't lay down Excalibur. That would only give Arthur a chance to claim it as his own. In this short time, I'd grown so accustomed in directing my magic with my hands that I felt at a disadvantage, even if I shouldn't. Magic could be directed in other ways after all.

I steadied my breathing, putting the pain out of my mind. I felt the wind and rain whip against my skin without doing any real damage. I could almost see the hints of Arthur's magic controlling the elements between us. But more importantly, I could sense the natural power coursing through every raindrop and every gust of wind.

On the other side of the courtyard, Arthur moved his hands in a circular motion. The rain and wind coalesced into a water spout, spinning faster and faster until it threatened to lose control. If it hit me, this would be over. I stepped forward and put out just enough intent to let nature know I didn't want to harm it.

Let me protect you.

The swirling water funnel froze midmotion as I stepped into it. Silence fell around me, but it wasn't oppressive. I was truly in the eye of the storm and I found a sense of peace I hadn't expected. The veins of Arthur's magic were clearer now. A vivid deep purple against the grey of the storm. The nearest thread lashed out the moment I got close.

A fresh bolt of lightning split the sky above me. Instead of striking me down, it struck the threads of my opponent's power, stripping them from the funnel. The rain and wind tightened their rotation and I could swear they slowed enough to caress my cheek before rippling outward to form a barrier.

Arthur hopped backward, scooped up the conjured sword into a single-handed hold on the hilt, and with his other hand conjured a fire ball. He used the blade like a bat to lob it at my torso. I parried the shot with little effort. I expected the fire to rebound on him, but it turned liquid, absorbed by Excalibur's blade. It sparkled across the visible spectrum of flames just as Arthur discarded his sword and channeled what must have been every ounce of his power into a single blow toward me.

I braced my back foot against the rock behind me and held Excalibur aloft, letting it deflect the power it couldn't absorb. Sweat drenched my body and the endorphins faded. The agony from my injury returned and my stomach lurched again the moment I repositioned myself. The water and wind continued to swirl between us as a barrier.

Don't give in now, Morgan. I reminded myself.

The energy building between us reached critical mass. I could almost see the outcome before it happened. I knew with this explosion of power; I'd get enough hits to end the match. We were seconds away from this whole ordeal *finally* being over. That still didn't give me the chance to protect myself as the blast filled the courtyard, sending me flying backward over the stone. I landed hard on my back, knocking the air from my lungs for what felt like the millionth time that afternoon.

The sky cleared as the energy dissipated. The base of my skull throbbed in time with my breathing from the impact. I was getting really tired of being thrown about like a fucking rag doll. My right hand suddenly stung and I looked down to see one of the gems in the hilt had dug a deep gash in my palm at some point. I almost felt offended that the sword so hellbent on defending me could have injured me at all. Somehow, I'd kept my grip on the sword even with the new injury. On instinct, my left hand tried to reach over to stop the bleeding, but fresh pain burned through me with the movement. My vision greyed at the edges from the pain and I inhaled short breaths through my nose until it went away. Coughing, I forced myself to roll onto my good shoulder and lever myself up to a seated position. Across the courtyard, Arthur lay on the ground, every part of his uniform that could signal a hit was alight and sparkling with lime-colored energy.

"Match and tournament go to Miss le Fey," the referee announced, failing to hide the utter shock in his tone.

Cheers erupted all around me as onlookers began chanting my name. Relief washed over me as I was about ready to collapse where I sat. I was vaguely aware of footfalls on the ground as Gethin and Emerys approached.

"Fuck," I grunted as Gethin tried to ease me up by my broken arm.

"Sorry," he said softly, producing a length of bandage to secure my arm to my chest until it could be assessed properly.

"This is not yet finished," Emerys said in my ear as I trudged across the grounds to where Arthur and the queen stood.

He bore fresh cuts and bruises, but that was the least shocking thing about the man now standing across from me. The illusion he'd been wearing had vanished and the cheers suddenly turned to gasps. Beside him the queen blinked, as if coming out of a daze. She studied me for a moment before turning to look at Arthur.

"You are not my son," she declared. "You are an imposter!"

Arthur took a few steps back. "I was never yours, Your Majesty," he said, casting his gaze up to the second spectator box where the fae royalty sat. "*Semper virtutis et gloriae.*"

I'd seen that phrase on the pins of some of the fae participants. He ripped the Camelot pin from his uniform, tossing it on the ground at his feet. Chaos erupted in the stands as all eyes fell on the spectator box. It was empty. Arthur's expression shifted momentarily to one of panic, before hardening into one of resolve. Arthur made a run for the nearest exit. He might be stronger than most other people in the tournament, but even his stamina had been challenged by the last five hours. And it appeared whatever I'd done to disrupt his control of the elements earlier was having a prolonged effect on his powers. He waved his hands in front of him, but nothing happened. I couldn't even feel a hint of power trying to coalesce to serve his intention.

"Seize him!" The queen's voice needed no amplification as she gave the order. "You have much to answer for."

Guards bearing Camelot's crest on their dress uniforms appeared, tackling Arthur to the ground. Even as they hauled him away, I could see the conflict warring on the queen's face. I could even see some of the guards hesitate to bind his hands behind his back. In a sense, I couldn't blame them. Until this moment, he'd been the heir to the throne. For all I knew, they'd grown up with him.

It still didn't give him the right to try and steal a throne that wasn't his. But could I really claim it as mine? I'd beaten him in this damn tournament, I'd freed Excalibur, but I wasn't a princess.

"Come with me," the queen said, drawing my attention. She looked over my right shoulder at Emerys. "It appears we have much to discuss."

TWENTY

Somehow, I made it out of the courtyard and into the castle proper under my own power. However, the moment we were hidden from the view of the masses, my legs gave out and I slammed to my knees. A jolt of pain seared up my broken arm and I bit down hard on my tongue to keep from swearing in front of the queen.

"She needs a doctor," Gethin said.

I gazed up at the woman I still couldn't bring myself to call mother through tears. The queen's hardness and fear melted a little. "Yes, of course. Help her up gently."

Two more guardsmen appeared and eased me back to my feet. One went so far as to let me drape my right arm around his shoulders. Together, we made a bizarre procession through a grand receiving hall, past a set of ornately carved wooden doors, and down a long corridor to a sitting room. The furniture was all upholstered in pale purples and blues. I eased into one of the hard-backed chairs and grimaced as my blood instantly stained the fabric.

"Sorry," I offered, not meeting the queen's gaze.

"It's just a chair," she answered. She turned to the guards with orders. "Fetch the doctor and find some clean clothes. She's going to need to change."

They each gave a stiff salute before hurrying out of the room. That left the queen and I flanked by Gethin and Emerys. As we waited for the doctor to arrive, I marveled at just how quiet the room was.

"Morgan, you can let go now," Gethin whispered.

It was only then I felt his fingers on my right hand, trying to pry the sword free from my grasp. My whole body shook at the thought of letting it go.

"No one should have been able to pull that sword free, not even me," the queen said, addressing Emerys.

"No one, but the true Pendragon heir," Emerys corrected. "And she has come home at last."

The queen studied my face and then her gaze settled on the sword beside me. The hilt was a garish mixture of vibrant blue gems stained a dark purple from the wound on my hand and some from the punctured skin and muscle in my other arm. Some blood had even seeped down along the blade.

"Tell me, do you know the history of this sword?" She dragged a chair to sit across from me.

"It's supposed to belong to the ruler of this kingdom," I answered. "And it's magic is somehow linked to Camelot's royal family bloodline."

"And you believe that includes you?"

"You're the one who knows how it all works better than me. Would it have allowed me to free it if I wasn't the right person?"

"She has a point," Emerys said.

"And the entire time I've been here, I've felt this pull forcing me to it. It was like some sort of beacon or something, going off in my head every time I got near it. Magic is in everything and that's what was calling to me. In my world, the one Nim took me to as a baby, I grew up terrible at magic. Nothing I did went right. But the minute I got here, it was like everything clicked. I was meant to be here and the magic of this place knows it," I explained.

"Magic can be faked," the queen murmured.

"The sword can tell if a person's a Pendragon based on blood, right?" I said, trying to sit up straighter. The queen nodded mutely. "I've bled all over this thing. If I wasn't actually a Pendragon I think we'd know by now."

My right hand shook as I peeled my fingers from around the hilt and offered it to her. I held it out, blade down. "Take it back if you don't believe me."

I didn't expect her to take me up on the offer to reclaim a bloodied weapon, but she extended her hand and it floated over to her, recognizing her claim to it as well. She laid it on the floor between us.

"I don't know how much you know about my husband," she started.

"I'm afraid I don't know much of anything," I replied, mentally counting the seconds that had gone by without receiving medical aid.

"He died not long before Ar—I mean ... you were born. I was grieving that loss when I went into labor. It was all such a blur." When she looked up, unshed tears sparkled in her eyes, hanging thick on her upper lashes. "I was so blinded by that loss. I didn't fully understand what was happening."

"I don't blame you." The words came out before I knew I'd even thought them.

She turned her attention back to Emerys. "But you do. And you have a right to. You have advised this family for far longer than I have been on this earth and I should have trusted you when you told me something was wrong."

Emerys reached out and grasped the queen's hands. "I know what it is to lose the love of your life. I remember that pain as if it were yesterday myself. I am only sorry I could not provide proof to break their hold over you."

The realization that my father had died before my birth hit me a few moments later. Oddly, I'd never much wondered about him. As a child, I'd always wondered what my mother had been like. Maybe because Aunt Nim's stories had always focused on the fact that the queen was the one who held the power here. To her, men weren't important. Despite that, I opened my mouth to ask the question that sat on the tip of my tongue. But I caught myself. We would have plenty of time to go down memory lane and share family stories when I wasn't about to pass out from my injuries.

"What happens now?" I shifted my position in the seat and hot pinpricks danced up my left shoulder. "To Arthur, I mean."

"We will have to determine Arthur's culpability. He will be held on trial and the coronation will be cancelled." The resigned expression on the queen's face sent pangs of guilt lancing through my chest.

"I would advise holding off on announcing Morgan as the rightful heir until matters can be settled," Emerys said.

"Matters?" I quipped. "What's that mean exactly?"

"As Ingrid noted, magic can be fabricated. You'll need to undergo a genetic test to conclusively prove for the masses that you are who we claim you to be."

"Great. Whenever your bloody doctor gets off his arse and arrives, he can take a DNA sample."

The door to the sitting room eased open and a man walked in at a leisurely stroll. I spied the medical bag in his hand and the nonchalant manner in which he moved only intensified the pain I was in, souring my mood even more.

"I trust you saw the match," the queen said in a low tone.

"I did, Your Highness."

"Please tend to Miss le Fey."

I wanted to bristle at her formality, but we weren't on a first name basis yet. After all, we were still strangers. He pivoted, took one look at me, and made an undignified gulp. "I can bandage the hand laceration, but she needs a proper surgeon to set that arm."

I bit down hard on my tongue to keep from crudely pointing out I could have told him that. I allowed him to examine my right hand and I did my best to stay conscious as he cleaned the wound and had me flex my fingers to ensure no tendons or ligaments had been damaged.

"You are a very lucky young woman," the doctor said as he secured the bandage around my hand.

"Don't feel very lucky ..." I mumbled, my words slurring together as the last vestiges of adrenaline evaporated and my surroundings went dark.

I CAME TO WITH A START. I expected to be in agony from the sudden jerking motion, but I found something soft and padded beneath my left arm. It was difficult to open my eyes, but not from being exhausted. My whole body felt almost weightless.

"Morgan, you awake?" Gethin's voice came from somewhere close by.

That was nice of him to come check on me. Slowly, the memory of the doctor's examination came flooding back to me. I forced my eyes open and found myself in a bedroom rather than the sitting room. The queen, Emerys, and the doctor were nowhere to be seen. I turned my head to find Gethin seated at the right hand side of the bed, worry lines creasing his forehead. He relaxed a little when our gazes met.

Well, I clearly wasn't dead. That was a good sign. I tried to push myself up into a sitting position in the bed and flailed. Gethin was out of his chair, easing me up and repositioning the pillows before I could ask for help. I took stock of my other injuries. My left arm was bandaged from elbow to shoulder and pinned against my chest in a sling.

"How long was I out?" I croaked.

"They got you into surgery pretty fast after you passed out. You'll have a bit of a scar, but they think you'll have full use of your arm again with some rehab."

I let out a snort. "A kingdom full of magic and modern medicine rides to the rescue."

"I mean ... the queen's got a private healer, but I'm not sure she trusts you enough yet to call her in."

"Can't say I blame her."

As I rested against the pillows, a sense of longing washed over me. It was almost as if a piece of me was missing, as if someone had chopped off a hand or a foot and I was only now acknowledging it.

"What's wrong?" Gethin straightened his glasses as he watched me, hawklike in his attempt to anticipate my needs.

"Nothing. Just worn out and overwhelmed," I lied.

Just then, I spotted a tray of food on the small, wheeled table behind him. "Please tell me you made me something to eat. I can't stand hospital rations."

That brightened my friend's demeanor considerably. "I couldn't let them give you boring food, so of course I made you a little something. I'd planned for you to be eating it at the tournament celebration, not in a hospital room."

He wheeled over the food and I sat for a solid five minutes just enjoying the aroma of the meal he'd prepared. Eating it was a bit more difficult with my injured hand, but I managed.

"So, where's Emerys and the queen?" I asked around a mouthful of pot roast and potatoes.

"They've been convening since you passed out. Or I guess catching up. They kicked me out honestly."

"Do you know if they took the DNA sample?"

"Yeah, it's being tested now through normal

means. Less chance people will contest it if there's science behind it."

"I still can't believe I actually did it. Won the tournament, and claimed Excalibur."

"You were brilliant," he boasted.

"What are people saying? After Arthur got arrested and they just whisked me away?"

"There's been speculation about whether Arthur was somehow replaced or if he's been a spy the whole time. And lots of questions about how you managed to free Excalibur. You may have been an unknown entity coming into this, but you've lost your anonymity."

"I suppose they'll just cancel the rest of the tournament ceremony," I said, breathing a little easier.

The door opened and Emerys appeared, looking far less anxious to be seen by people than she had all week. "I am glad to see you are on the mend. They'll keep the ceremony brief. Present you with the victor's trophy and then allow you to return to convalesce."

"People can't really be bothered with seeing me get some bloody trophy after everything that just happened," I argued.

"This tournament is more political than you realize. Tension may be rising with the Seelie court and standing on ceremony will give people a sense of normalcy. It will put them more at ease."

"Fine," I muttered.

"You'll have a few more hours' rest and then we'll go."

I flopped back onto the pile of pillows. "Everything's going to change now," I sighed.

"Yes, it is. You have begun to take hold of the destiny that awaits you, Morgan Pendragon," Emerys said, her tone turning formal.

That was enough to force me upright again. "What'd you call me?"

"You are a Pendragon by birth and by right. You should get used to people referring to you as such."

"I'm not changing my name," I argued.

"The name you were given falsely links you to those who sought to disrupt this kingdom's stability."

"Aunt Nim gave me that name and I won't change it. I don't give a fuck if she was fae or human. She's my family and I will not tarnish her memory by abandoning that connection."

"Emerys do not push her," the queen said, stepping into the room. She gestured to both Emerys and Gethin. "I would like a moment alone with Morgan."

Gethin straightened and did as he was told. Yet the way his lips twitched into a frown suggested he was only doing so because the leader of his kingdom gave him a direct order. Once we were alone, the queen settled onto the edge of the bed and tentatively reached out to take my right hand.

"I thought of all people you'd agree with Emerys," I said.

"I can see a reason for maintaining the name you grew up with, especially if you must travel between kingdoms. But she is right. You will formally be known by your family name."

"So, you believe that I'm your daughter?"

"I think a part of me knew it the moment Excalibur left the stone. I spent so long trying to convince myself that the sword had been locked within it as a test all because we'd never had a boy born to the family line. But I realize now that wasn't the case. It could sense what I couldn't see and was protecting itself and our family's legacy." She let out a breath. "Even still, a part of me doesn't believe this is real."

"I know the feeling. Aunt Nim spent my entire childhood telling me stories about this place, trying to prepare me for when I came back. At some point, I stopped believing it was ever real. But ... now I'm living what she talked about and I don't know if I'm ready to believe that it's real."

"As much as I wish I could have been there in your childhood, I am grateful you had someone who kept this place alive in your heart, even in some small way."

"She was fae, you know. Seelie."

"Emerys explained everything. We must try very hard not to judge a people by the actions of a few. Although I must admit I am finding it incredibly difficult today."

"I'm right there with you."

She offered me a genuine smile. "I am sorry it took so much pain to find one another again. I only hope we can build something akin to a relationship. I've never had a daughter, but I very much look forward to having one."

She stood and offered me her hand. "Come, let's get you crowned as victor of the tournament."

By some small mercy, I was able to change out of the hospital gown into something resembling normal clothes. My arm still hurt when I moved, but it wasn't the same searing pain as before. I didn't expect the queen to escort me back out to the courtyard and yet she did, head held high.

They'd erected a small stage with a podium,

much like they'd done at the opening ceremony. She moved to stand behind it after gesturing for me to stand to her left. The stadium seating still remained packed. Either everyone had come back for this or they'd all just waited for the last few hours to find out what would happen next.

"Well, it has certainly been an eventful tournament," the queen began, her voice amplified throughout the space. "It is my honor to present the victor of this year's challenge to Morgan le Fey. She brings honor and dedication to Camelot's name. *Materna Magica*."

"*Materna Magica*," a chorus of voices echoed back.

I didn't know what else lay ahead of me, but I knew I wasn't alone. I might not be ready to be Morgan Pendragon, but Morgan le Fey was a badass. And even if it only lasted for this brief moment in time, I was ready to take on anything.

QUICK AUTHOR'S NOTE

I HAD an absolute blast writing this story. It was such a departure from what I've written in the past.

I will admit, at first I was a little nervous because this book didn't really have a core mystery to solve and Morgan was a big step away from the law enforcement characters I'd written in this universe. But, in the end, I feel like it turned out exceptionally well.

I liked that Morgan wasn't the same archetype as Ezri or Kayla, yet she fit right in with them in my mind. She has her own journey to go on as she fights to claim her destiny and it's going to be an exciting one!

Speaking of that journey, while I had a lot of fun beginning to craft and explore Camelot in this first book, book two, Her Amber Chalice, brings us back to the familiar Seasons of Magic world (or at least our realm).

Turn the page for a look at Her Amber Chalice...

HER AMBER CHALICE

Reclaiming her throne is only the beginning...

Morgan le Fey may have returned to modern-day Camelot, but settling into her new role as heir apparent is anything but easy. A simple witch at heart, the scrutiny of her every move proves stifling. When the threat of war looms over her newfound home, Morgan leaps at the chance to act.

Morgan's magic leads her back to the streets of London on the hunt for the Holy Grail. Her return to the city also reunites her with her childhood friend and her first witch knight. Along the way, Morgan struggles to blend her old life with the destiny unfolding before her.

Their search takes them from the Tower of London to ancient abbeys and through the city's magical underbelly. The closer Morgan and her companions get to unearthing the Grail's true location, the more danger lurks.

Even if Morgan can lay hands on the mythical object, will she be able to control its power and keep it from falling into enemy hands? Or will her first quest end in tragedy?

Scan the QR code to get your copy of Her Amber Chalice.

About the Author

Sarah Biglow is a *USA Today* bestselling author. She lives in Massachusetts with her husband and son. She is a licensed attorney and spends her days combatting employment discrimination as an Investigator with the Massachusetts Commission Against Discrimination.

You can find an up-to-date list of all my books here